WHO KILLED
ROGER ACKROYD?

WHO KILLED ROGER ACKROYD?

The Mystery Behind the Agatha Christie Mystery

PIERRE BAYARD

Translated by Carol Cosman

THE NEW PRESS

NEW YORK

Originally published as *Qui a tué Roger Ackroyd?* by Editions de Minuit

Published in the United States by The New Press, New York, 2000
Distributed by W.W. Norton & Company, Inc., New York

LIBRARY OF CONGRESS CATALOGING-IN-PUBLICATION DATA
Bayard, Pierre.
    [Qui a tué Roger Ackroyd? English]
    Who killed Roger Ackroyd? : the mystery behind the Agatha Christie
mystery / Pierre Bayard ; translated by Carol Cosman.
        p.   cm.
    ISBN 1-56584-579-X (hc.)
    Includes bibliographical references (pp. 147–160).
    1. Christie, Agatha, 1890–1976. Murder of Roger Ackroyd.
    2. Psychoanalysis and literature—England—History—20th century.
    3. Detective and mystery stories, English—History and criticism.
    4. Detective and mystery stories—Authorship. 5. Poirot, Hercule
(Fictitious character). I. Cosman, Carol, II. Title.

PR6005.H66 M853313 2000
823'.912—dc21
                                                            99–054834

The New Press was established in 1990 as a not-for-profit alternative to the
large, commercial publishing houses currently dominating the book publishing industry. The New Press operates in the public interest rather than for
private gain, and is committed to publishing, in innovative ways, works of
educational, cultural, and community value that are often deemed insuffi-
ciently profitable.

The New Press
450 West 41st Street, 6th Floor
New York, NY 10036

www.thenewpress.com

Printed in the United States of America

9 8 7 6 5 4 3 2 1

CONTENTS

PROLOGUE

Many of today's readers know who killed Roger Ackroyd. Lovers of detective fiction, in particular, know the organizing principle of Agatha Christie's novel *The Murder of Roger Ackroyd* and can give the correct answer: The murderer is the narrator. The best informed can even supply his name: Dr. Sheppard.

The originality of Christie's method has made this work hugely successful, one of the most famous novels in literary history. The book's fate transcends the boundaries of the detective genre, and numerous studies in the humanities have used it to deal with theoretical problems posed by its singular construction.[1]

Though the novel instantly established Agatha Christie's celebrity, its publication was not unanimously acclaimed. Several reviews at the time—echoed more recently—suggested that by making the narrator the murderer, the novelist had violated the tacit pact between the author of a detective novel and her public—that she had, in fact, cheated.[2]

Curiously, admirers and detractors of the book agree on the crucial point: No one dreams of doubting Dr. Sheppard's guilt. So before asking ourselves whether it is legitimate to conceal the murderer behind the narrator or not, it seems wise to ask ourselves if the guilty party is really the person named by the investigation.

This is the task at hand: We shall disengage ourselves from popular opinion, which holds that Dr. Sheppard is the killer, and attempt to steer a third course between admiration and reproach. While accepting no previous assumptions, we shall be satisfied with answering the simple question: Who killed Roger Ackroyd?

*   *   *

The drawback of the book's success is that the aesthetic beauty of its method tends to eclipse the mystery plot. Fascinated by Agatha Christie's ingenious concealment of the truth, the reader is liable to be distracted from the criminal question and forget to examine whether the proposed solution is plausible. Moreover, this solution is dispatched in just a few pages by a Hercule Poirot so enamored of his own inventiveness that he neglects the many problems posed by such a complex mystery.

Our first concern, then, is with rigor. A detective novel, at least when it is part of the genre in which Agatha Christie works, is bound to obey a seamless logic. This first concern is tied to the question of justice: If we discover that Dr. Sheppard is not the murderer, a judicial error would have been caused by Hercule Poirot and all those who accepted his solution unprotestingly.

So we propose to review every aspect of the case in detail by examining as objectively as possible whether Hercule Poirot's solution is valid, and whether we can be sure that Dr. Sheppard committed the murder. Dedicated to the rereading of a detective novel, this book finds itself necessarily taking the shape of a detective novel as well, one that will lead the reader in its final pages toward what seems the more likely solution.

But this book is not only a detective novel about a detective novel. It has a second, more theoretical purpose that concerns delusion, and in particular the delusion of interpretation. This issue is deeply connected to our work here. To challenge Hercule Poirot's solution is to accuse him of being delusional, an accusation made, in fact, by the dumbfounded Dr. Sheppard when Poirot triumphantly announces the result of his reflections.

At the same time, of course, we risk constructing a delusional reading ourselves, since we are following a procedure identical to Poirot's, consisting of a minute examination of the clues, an interpretation of the facts, and an organization of our deductions into a harmonious and coherent whole.

It would not be wrong, then, to say that this book is dedicated to the experimental construction of a delusional reading built on the same principles as Poirot's, mirroring and attempting to mimic his thought processes. Such a reading is not intrinsically mad, but is certainly shot through at moments, like all great systematic delusions, with an invisible streak of lunacy.

Constructing a delusion at least offers one advantage: It allows us an alternative way of reflecting on a true reading. Often one poses the question in the most traditional manner, by wondering *how to approach the true*. It may be of interest, however, to pose the question from another angle and to wonder, rather, *how to approach the false* by exploring it from within, thus rendering it familiar.

If such a reading is to be meaningful, however, its implications should be significant, particularly for other works by Agatha Christie and by other writers of detective novels, whose suspicious readers sometimes have the feeling that the murderer has managed to escape the investigator's shrewd eye. While the detective novel is often thought to require a single reading, our proposal has the benefit of inviting us to review a number of dubious cases and to set off on the trail of unpunished criminals.[3]

But, in addition, numerous literary deaths—and not only those in detective fiction—would merit reconsideration. Who has ever seriously wondered, for example, about the strange fatal epidemics that strike the heroes of La Fontaine's fables? Are we so certain that the *dame aux camélias* died a natural death? Is it unthinkable that Madame Bovary might have been murdered? And what do we really know about the death of Bergotte?

Quite apart from the problem of suspect deaths, numerous

accepted literary facts would benefit in all sorts of ways from being recast or illuminated from another perspective. Perhaps it is time to ask ourselves what happened to Madame de Merteuil, in *Les Liaisons dangereuses* after her flight to Holland. What is the real identity of Balzac's putative Colonel Chabert? And who among all the suspected mine workers really unleashed the disaster in Zola's *Germinal*?

Many readers of fictional texts have at times experienced the disagreeable impression that they are being kept in the dark. Perhaps this book will help to unearth buried secrets beyond those in the work of Agatha Christie that disturb the transparency of reading, examining under what conditions it is possible, without distorting the aims of the works, to helpfully extend the information about them that we already possess.

CAST OF CHARACTERS

JAMES SHEPPARD, village doctor of King's Abbot, bachelor, narrator of the story.

CAROLINE SHEPPARD, James's sister, no profession, spinster. Lives with her brother. Known for her curiosity, which she sustains through a network of informers in the village.

ROGER ACKROYD, country gentleman. Discovered murdered after receiving a letter in which his mistress, Mrs. Farrars, who subsequently committed suicide, revealed to him the name of the person who had been blackmailing her for a year by threatening to disclose to the police that she had murdered her husband.

MRS. CECIL ACKROYD, widow of Roger Ackroyd's brother Cecil; recently arrived from Canada with her daughter, Flora.

FLORA ACKROYD, daughter of Mrs. Cecil Ackroyd and Roger Ackroyd's niece.

RALPH PATON, son of Roger Ackroyd's first wife; treated by Ackroyd like his own son. Revealed at the end of the book, thanks to Hercule Poirot, to be the husband of Ursula Bourne, parlormaid.

HECTOR BLUNT, professional big-game hunter passing through King's Abbot; friend of Roger Ackroyd, who puts him up during his visits to England.

GEOFFREY RAYMOND, Roger Ackroyd's personal secretary.

PARKER, Roger Ackroyd's butler.

ELIZABETH RUSSELL, Roger Ackroyd's housekeeper. Rumored in the village to have matrimonial designs on him; these are subsequently quashed by the arrival of Mrs. Cecil Ackroyd and Flora Ackroyd, and especially by the romantic relationship between Roger Ackroyd and Mrs. Farrars. Mother of Charles Kent.

CHARLES KENT, son of Elizabeth Russell. Identity discovered by Hercule Poirot. Marginal drug addict. Encountered by Sheppard as Sheppard leaves Roger Ackroyd's estate on the evening of the murder; Sheppard is unable to identify him.

HERCULE POIROT, retired private detective.

WHO KILLED
ROGER ACKROYD?

PART I

INVESTIGATION

CHAPTER 1

THE MURDER

Replaying the investigation into the death of Roger Ackroyd involves conveying the chief elements of the story to the reader. Obviously, it would be ideal if every reader had the time to read or reread Agatha Christie's novel *The Murder of Roger Ackroyd*. But, due to the difficulty of satisfying this requirement, our investigation will be prefaced by a precise and objective exposition of the facts insofar as this is possible.[1]

The story is set in a little village in rural England, King's Abbot, whose resident physician, and the narrator of the book, is a Dr. Sheppard. It begins with these words: "Mrs. Ferrars died on the night of the 16th–17th September—a Thursday. I was sent for at eight o'clock on the morning of Friday the 17th. There was nothing to be done. She had been dead some hours" (I, 11).

Because of his position as narrator, Dr. Sheppard's defining features are not given to us directly but are revealed progressively in the course of the action. He is a bachelor who devotes most of his time to medicine, but he is also enamored of gardening and tinkering with mechanical devices. He seems to be a steady man, rather impassive by nature, who lives with his sister Caroline. The doctor's narrative introduces her as a spinster of indeterminate age, whose principal characteristic is an intense curiosity and whose chief occupation is gossip. Both are sustained by the various events of village life and by information obtained from a close network of servants and tradesmen:

> Caroline can do any amount of finding out by sitting placidly at home. I don't know how she manages it, but

there it is. I suspect that the servants and the tradesmen constitute her Intelligence Corps. When she goes out, it is not to gather information, but to spread it. At that, too, she is amazingly expert (I, 11–12).

As proof of Caroline's effectiveness, by the time Dr. Sheppard returns home from his discovery of Mrs. Ferrars' death, his sister already knows about it:

> "You've had an early call," remarked Caroline.
> "Yes," I said. "King's Paddock. Mrs. Ferrars."
> "I know," said my sister.
> "How did you know?"
> "Annie told me."
> Annie is the house parlormaid. A nice girl, but an inveterate talker.
> There was a pause. I continued to eat eggs and bacon. My sister's nose, which is long and thin, quivered a little at the tip, as it always does when she is interested or excited over anything. "Well?" she demanded.
> "A bad business. Nothing to be done. Must have died in her sleep."
> "I know," said my sister again.
> This time I was annoyed. "You can't know," I snapped. "I didn't know myself until I got there, and I haven't mentioned it to a soul yet. If that girl Annie knows, she must be clairvoyant."
> "It wasn't Annie who told me. It was the milkman. He had it from the Ferrars's cook" (I, 12–13).

Caroline then suggests, against her brother's public position, that Mrs. Ferrars committed suicide out of remorse for having poisoned her husband. He had died a year before, of apparently natural causes, but Caroline had always been convinced that murder was involved. Sharing his sister's opinion ("It's odd how, when you have a secret belief of your own which you do not wish to acknowledge, the voicing of it by some one else will rouse you to a fury of denial" [I,14]), but refusing to say so, the doctor decides not to argue.

A short while later, Sheppard encounters Roger Ackroyd in the street. "A man more impossibly like a country squire than any country squire could really be" (I, 16), Roger Ackroyd is the soul of King's Abbot. About fifty years old and very rich, he lives with his family in one of the village's two important houses, Fernly Park. He was married briefly when he was a young man to a woman by the name of Paton, a widow whose child, Ralph, Roger Ackroyd has always treated like his own son and raised as such. Ralph is twenty-five years old at this time and, since he is perpetually short of money, a considerable source of worry to his adoptive father.

Let's pause a moment at Fernly Park and reflect on its residents, who include most of the suspects in the book. With the exception of Ralph, Fernly Park is home to two other members of Roger Ackroyd's family who have settled there only recently: Mrs. Cecil Ackroyd, a sister-in-law who is the "widow of Ackroyd's ne'er-do-well younger brother" (II,18), and her daughter, Flora, both of whom arrived from Canada. Both ladies are constantly in need of money and are financially dependent on Roger Ackroyd, who hopes that Ralph and Flora will marry. As the story opens a match is in progess between the two young people.

Now let's move on to the house staff. Numerous housekeepers have succeeded one another, the most recent being Elizabeth Russell, who has run things for five years. She might have managed to marry Roger Ackroyd if he had not fallen in love with Mrs. Ferrars. The arrival of Mrs. Cecil Ackroyd and Flora also seems to have played a role in checking Elizabeth Russell's ambitions.

The second crucial character among the servants is a parlormaid named Ursula Bourne, dismissed shortly before Ackroyd's death. She will be revealed, at the end of the book, to be the wife of Ralph Paton; they had married without telling anyone, including Roger Ackroyd and Flora. It was upon discovering this secret union that Ackroyd fired Ursula Bourne/Paton.

Among the staff we must also single out Parker, because of both his important role in discovering the murder and his past as a blackmailer. After conducting his investigation, Poirot reveals that Parker was blackmailing his previous employer— making him one of the chief suspects.

Roger Ackroyd's house includes two more occupants: first, his personal secretary, a self-effacing young man named Geoffrey Raymond, and a friend, the well-known big-game hunter Major Hector Blunt. Blunt, a temporary visitor to Ackroyd's estate where he stays on his trips to England, will fall in love with Flora.

All these characters are introduced at the beginning of the book. One other, however, equally connected to Fernly Park, is not: Charles Kent, a social misfit and drug addict, and therefore a prime suspect. Kent turns out to be the stranger whom Dr. Sheppard encounters on the night of the murder as he leaves Roger Ackroyd's estate. Thanks to Hercule Poirot's acumen, the police learn that Kent is Elizabeth Russell's son.

When Dr. Sheppard meets Roger Ackroyd in the village, Ackroyd seems devastated by the death of Mrs. Ferrars, his mistress, but preoccupied with other matters. He has secrets to divulge, and, unable to speak freely to Sheppard in the street, asks the doctor to stop by that evening.

The narrator then gives us a detailed account of his day. The morning is devoted to his patients. After lunch, he does some gardening until he is almost hit on the head by a "vegetable marrow" (perhaps a pumpkin) lobbed over the fence by his new neighbor in a fit of bad temper over the state of his own garden. This is how Dr. Sheppard makes the acquaintance of

Hercule Poirot, who, although full of apology, does not inform the doctor of his profession on this first meeting. Dr. Sheppard then pays a visit to his friend Ralph Paton, Ackroyd's stepson, who is staying, he has learned, at the village inn, the Three Boars. He spends the later afternoon at home, then heads toward Ackroyd's house where he has been invited for dinner at seven-thirty.

At Fernly Park, Sheppard is welcomed by Parker, the butler, and by Ackroyd's secretary, Geoffrey Raymond. About to enter the drawing room, Sheppard hears an odd noise coming from inside. Upon entering, Sheppard encounters Miss Russell, the housekeeper, who is just leaving. He also notices that the long French doors to the terrace did not apparently cause the noise, but that the closing of the glass top of a "silver table" containing old curios was the source of the mysterious sound.

At dinner, Sheppard finds several of the characters already introduced, namely Roger Ackroyd himself, Mrs. Cecil Ackroyd, his niece Flora, Parker, Geoffrey Raymond, and Major Blunt. The mood is rather gloomy. Immediately after dinner Sheppard meets privately with Ackroyd in his study to hear the revelations hinted at that morning.

Evidently so distressed that he repeatedly checks for the presence of spies and eavesdroppers, Ackroyd begins by asking Sheppard, who had formerly cared for Mr. Ferrars, if he ever thought Ferrars might have been poisoned. Ackroyd then reveals that Ferrars was murdered by his wife. The previous evening she had proposed marriage and confessed to Ackroyd, much to his amazement, that she had killed her husband to be free of him. But Mrs. Ferrars was not satisfied with confessing her crime: she also revealed to Ackroyd—without naming names—that for the past year she had been the victim of blackmail. Ackroyd has a hunch, however, that before dying in despair at his obvious revulsion, Mrs. Ferrars left him a letter denouncing the blackmailer. He believes that her suicide was also an appeal for vengeance.

At this moment Parker, the butler, enters the study with the evening mail, which includes a blue envelope from Mrs. Ferrars. Ackroyd starts to read the letter aloud ("I leave to you the punishment of the person who has made my life hell upon earth for the last year. I would not tell you the name this afternoon, but I propose to write it to you now" [IV,47]), then interrupts himself, demanding that Sheppard leave the room, since this letter is personal. Sheppard pleads in vain to hear the rest.

Here we come to what is perhaps the most famous passage in the book—a passage thought to implicate Sheppard in the murder:

> Now Ackroyd is essentially pig-headed. The more you urge him to do a thing, the more determined he is not to do it. All my arguments were in vain.
>
> The letter had been brought in at twenty minutes to nine. It was just on ten minutes to nine when I left him, the letter still unread. I hesitated with my hand on the door handle, looking back and wondering if there was anything I had left undone. I could think of nothing. With a shake of the head I passed out and closed the door behind me (IV, 48).

Closing the study door, Sheppard encounters Parker, who appears to have been eavesdropping on the conversation and to whom Sheppard conveys Ackroyd's wish not to be disturbed. As he leaves the house, passing through the gates to the estate, the village clock strikes nine o'clock. He nearly collides with a man coming from the opposite direction (we learn at the end of the book that this is Charles Kent, Elizabeth Russell's son) who asks in a hoarse voice the way to Fernly Park. Returning home ten minutes later, Sheppard finds his sister Caroline and gives her an account of the evening. At a quarter past ten, the telephone rings. Sheppard takes the call, then shouts to Caroline as he prepares to leave: "Parker telephoning . . . from Fernly. They've just found Roger Ackroyd murdered" (IV, 49).

He then returns to Fernly Park, where he is welcomed by Parker, who is surprised to see him again and denies having telephoned. The two men head for Ackroyd's study. Since there is no sound coming from the locked room, Sheppard decides to force the door. Inside they discover Ackroyd's corpse with a dagger plunged into the neck: "Ackroyd was sitting as I had left him in the armchair before the fire. His head had fallen sideways, and clearly visible, just below the collar of his coat, was a shining piece of twisted metalwork" (V, 52). Sheppard then sends Parker to telephone the police, while he remains alone in the room: "Parker hurried away, still wiping his perspiring brow. I did what little had to be done" (V, 53). He notes that the blue envelope containing the name of the blackmailer has disappeared. The police arrive a few minutes later and the investigaton begins.

Before continuing our account, let us note that all the important characters in the book have been introduced. Of course, other transitory figures (for example, those on Ackroyd's staff or some of the investigators) will appear here and there, but the real protagonists of a detective novel are those in primary positions. The criminal cannot have a secondary role. The rules of the genre similarly exclude the possibility that the murderer is a stranger from the outside, such as a passing vagabond. This solution, favored by several characters in the book who are loath to discover a murderer in their midst, is not a possibility in the detective mystery.

This limitation of possibilities favors our plan. The murderer, whoever he is, figures among the characters we have just introduced. The dragnet now begins to close around him.

CHAPTER 2

THE INVESTIGATION

The investigation is officially headed by Inspector Raglan, soon joined by Hercule Poirot. Poirot is retired and, as already noted, living in the house next to the Sheppards. He becomes involved in the inquiries at the request of Flora Ackroyd and Caroline Sheppard, who ask him to intervene. The two women are afraid that the police may arrest Ralph Paton, for whom they feel sympathy and whom they consider incapable of murder. After advising them that if he undertakes the investigation, he will see it through to the end, Poirot then begins his own search, parallel to that of the police.

This traditional organization of the detective novel, which pits a doltish police inspector against a brilliant detective, offers us two investigations leading to different conclusions. While the police follow a classic line of argument producing a likely murderer, Hercule Poirot advances by means of unpredictable lines of argument toward an unexpected murderer. The two progressions obey disparate logical methods: The police operate in broad daylight while Poirot moves in shadow, allowing only a few puzzling clues to filter through until the final revelation.

After eliminating several false leads pointing to Parker or Elizabeth Russell's son Charles Kent, Inspector Raglan's investigation quickly brings him to suspect Ralph Paton. Indeed, everything points to the accusation of Ackroyd's stepson. Deeply in debt, he is the heir to the deceased's vast fortune. He acknowledges being on the property on the evening of the murder but denies having entered Ackroyd's study. More serious still, the gravel near his stepfather's windows bears the imprint of his shoes. Finally, he disappears after the murder, and is assumed to have fled. In short, he is the perfect suspect.

Hercule Poirot's investigation unfolds along two axes. The first consists of resolving a number of secondary mysteries that stymie other attempts. He is determined, for instance, to establish the truth about the time of the murder. Relying on the testimony of Flora Ackroyd, who verifies having seen her uncle alive at 9:45 P.M., the investigators figure that his death took place after this time. Poirot proves that the young woman, wishing to disguise a theft, has lied,[1] permitting the supposition that the murder took place well before.

Similarly, Poirot traces clues found in a summer house on Ackroyd's property to two couples among the characters who had met there on the night of the murder. Poirot reveals that the first couple, Ralph Paton and Ursula Bourne, were secretly married. They had met to decide what course to take after Ackroyd discovered their marriage and dismissed Ursula Bourne.[2] The second couple was Elizabeth Russell and Charles Kent, her son. They, too, met in the summer house the night of the murder, and it was Charles, who had come to ask for his mother's help, whom Sheppard encountered on leaving the estate.

All these plot twists, which Poirot resolves one by one, make the problem more complex and disturb the investigation by attracting our attention to suspects whom the detective considers guilty of only minor transgressions. In the same spirit he entertains, then rejects, the hypotheses that Parker the butler (already accused of blackmail in another affair), Charles Kent, or the stepson Ralph Paton may have committed the murder.

Though Hercule Poirot examines all the clues at his disposal, his attention very quickly fixes on a number of points neglected by the police and to which he obsessively returns throughout the book. These will serve as the basis of his conclusions.

The first clue is the telephone call alerting Sheppard to Ackroyd's death. The police have traced this call, placed not from the Ackroyd residence but from the village train station. Parker is therefore not its initiator, and Raglan comes up with no satisfying solution, except to think that the murderer was seized by a fit of madness. Poirot is convinced that a completely rational explanation for this telephone call exists, and that solving this problem will lead directly to the murderer.

The second clue is a displaced object. Thanks to Parker's testimony, Poirot discovers that a piece of furniture in the room where Ackroyd was murdered—a high-backed "grandfather" chair—has been moved slightly between the time when the corpse was discovered and the arrival of the police. He confers great importance on this detail, which seems secondary to the investigators. His first explanation is that the furniture was pushed back to hide the window. The second explanation will lead him to the murderer.

Poirot pays equal attention to how many pairs of shoes Ralph Paton had with him when he arrived at the Three Boars Inn. Sure that the young man is innocent, he hypothesizes that the real murderer borrowed Paton's shoes in order to leave misleading footprints in the gravel outside Ackroyd's windows. It must be assumed, then, that Paton—on his short visit to the village—had at least two pairs of shoes. (In fact, Paton had several pairs with him.) For this information, Poirot turns to Sheppard's sister Caroline, who activates her network of informers.

Poirot reveals his proposed solution in two stages. First, he employs the traditional ceremony concluding many of Agatha Christie's works: a gathering of the various suspects. Present are Mrs. Cecil Ackroyd, Flora Ackroyd, Major Blunt, Geoffrey Raymond, Ursula Bourne (Paton), Parker, Elizabeth Russell, and, of course, Dr. Sheppard. Several times before and during this gathering, Poirot states that the murderer is to be found in this group.

The meeting, which takes place at Poirot's residence, begins with the introduction of Ralph Paton's wife, Ursula Bourne, to the other participants, who have had no inkling of their secret marriage. Then Poirot comes back to the two mysterious meetings that took place in the summer house on Ackroyd's property on the evening of the crime, and to the different clues left at these meetings. He explains that the two couples met there in sequence: first Ralph Paton and his wife Ursula, and later, Elizabeth Russell and her son, Charles Kent.

Then Poirot stages an unexpected and theatrical conjuring. At the general request of the participants, eager to know Ralph Paton's whereabouts, Poirot gestures melodramatically toward the door, and the young man appears on the threshold. Poirot reveals that Paton was hidden in a nearby psychiatric hospital by Dr. Sheppard, whom he amicably reproaches for not telling him everything.

Noting that Ralph Paton has no serious alibi, Poirot observes that only one thing can still save him: The true murderer must confess. He addresses himself to that person in these terms: "I who speak to you—I know the murderer of Mr. Ackroyd is in this room now. It is to the murderer I speak. *Tomorrow the truth goes to Inspector Raglan.* You understand?" (XXIV, 241).

The heavy silence that follows is interrupted only by the arrival of Poirot's servant bringing the evening mail on a tray, from which Poirot takes a telegram before announcing that he is now certain of the murderer's identity. He then dismisses the group but asks Dr. Sheppard to stay behind for a moment.

Left alone with the inspector, Sheppard expresses his confusion and asks why Poirot didn't go directly to Inspector Raglan instead of giving the guilty party this elaborate warning. Doesn't he risk the murderer's escape? Poirot gravely replies that the guilty party has only one means of evasion at his disposal, one that does not lead to freedom. He offers to walk Sheppard through his investigation: "I will take you the way that I have traveled myself. Step by step you shall accompany me, and see for yourself that all the facts point indisputably to one person" (XXV, 243).

Poirot reviews the evidence that has attracted his attention: first, the telephone call announcing the murder. If Ralph Paton were the murderer, he observes, there would have been no reason for this communication; this argues for his innocence. The motive for this call, which results in the immediate discovery of the murder, was certainly to give the murderer a pretext to be there when the door to Ackroyd's study was opened, or on the scene soon after. This exonerates Parker, who would have been present in any case.

The second point is the displacement of the highbacked chair. Poirot observes that he is the only one to consider this detail significant. He reminds Sheppard that this chair was found between the door to Ackroyd's study and the window, but that it also hid a small table. He now believes that this table may have held an object that the murderer wanted to conceal from general view.

Pondering the nature of this object, Poirot comes up with the idea of a dictaphone and remembers that Ackroyd, shortly before the murder, had ordered and received one that has not been found. Should the murderer have wanted to conceal such a large item, he must have come with a "receptacle" big enough to carry it away discreetly, and therefore he would have been at the scene of the crime when the door to the study was opened.

Sheppard asks what point there was in removing the dictaphone, to which Poirot replies that the dictaphone served to mask the time of death by replaying a recording of Ackroyd's voice, giving the impression to those outside the study that he was still alive well after the presumed moment of his death— thereby giving the murderer an alibi. Thus, Poirot's profile of the murderer becomes more specific: He must have known that Ackroyd had bought a dictaphone, and he must have some understanding of mechanical devices.

Poirot's final observations concern, first, the footprints left in front of the study windows, and second, the theft of the dagger from the silver table. If the murderer is not Ralph Paton, he must have had time to go to the Three Boars to borrow a pair of his shoes. Also, the murderer must have had the opportunity to steal the dagger on the evening of the murder.

Bringing all these elements together leads Poirot to his accusatory conclusion:

> Let us recapitulate—now that all is clear. A person who was at the Three Boars earlier that day, a person who knew Ackroyd well enough to know that he had purchased a dictaphone, a person who was of a mechanical turn of mind, who had the opportunity to take the dagger from the silver table before Miss Flora arrived, who had with him a receptacle suitable for hiding the dictaphone—such as a black bag, and who had the study to himself for a few minutes after the crime was discovered while Parker was telephoning for the police. In fact—*Dr. Sheppard!*" (XXV, 248–249)

In the presence of the stupefied Dr. Sheppard, Poirot elaborates. His attention was first attracted by a small discrepancy in timing. Sheppard always claimed that he had left Ackroyd's house at ten minutes to nine—a claim confirmed by Parker—and had stepped out of the gate to the estate at nine o'clock. Yet everyone agrees that it takes only five minutes to cover this ground. What could explain this discrepancy?

According to this reading of the facts, then, Sheppard kills Ackroyd just before leaving his study, where he has made sure to leave the window open and set the dictaphone to turn on at nine-thirty. Once outside the house, he slips on Paton's shoes—

which he had stolen that afternoon at the inn—and leaves footprints under the windows. His aim, of course, is to implicate Paton. This is also why he tries to conceal the young man, making him even more suspect in the eyes of the police.

In Poirot's explanation, the two mysteries of the telephone call and the displacement of the highbacked chair are connected to the dictaphone. The telephone call was made from King Abbot's train station by a patient of Sheppard's—a steward about to embark on an ocean voyage. Apparently the doctor had entrusted the steward with a letter to another patient and asked the man to phone him at ten o'clock the evening of the murder, with that patient's reply. This call allowed him, after telling his sister that the call was from Parker, to return to Ackroyd's home and to be present when the study was opened so he could recover the dictaphone.

In the study after the discovery of the body, having sent the butler to call the police, Sheppard places the dictaphone in his black bag and returns the highbacked chair to its usual place.

To Sheppard's question regarding his purported motive, Poirot accuses him of being the blackmailer who was persecuting Mrs. Ferrars following her poisoning of her husband, and thus of fearing Ackroyd's reaction to this discovery. Poirot had asked himself who would be better positioned than Mr. Ferrars' doctor to know the cause of that man's death? But the blackmail money does Sheppard little good, as he loses most of it in fruitless speculations.

Finished with his demonstration, Poirot proposes that out of regard for Caroline, he will give Sheppard a way out by allowing him to commit suicide, warning him that it is useless to try and get rid of the detective the way he got rid of Ackroyd: "It would be most unwise on your part to attempt to silence me as you silenced M. Ackroyd. That kind of business does not succeed against Hercule Poirot, you understand" (XXVI, 252).

The two men take leave of each other very politely and the

book ends with four pages in which Dr. Sheppard, after quickly touching on Ackroyd's death once more, suggests that he has decided to commit suicide and expresses his regret that Hercule Poirot had chosen this village for his retirement: "But I wish Hercule Poirot had never retired from work and come here to grow vegetable marrows" (XXVII, 255).

CHAPTER 3

THE VAN DINE PRINCIPLE

Few writers have mined the eminently Freudian question of psychic blindness as systematically as Agatha Christie. *Why don't we see?* Agatha Christie poses this question in all her plots, but also relates the question to the reader, for beyond the detective story, every book tells the same tale about the blindness of *those who read it*.

The type of blindness we are dealing with here is of interest to psychoanalysis, which naturally attends to things that escape consciousness. In this respect, Agatha Christie's work *displays* the unconscious, not by calling for the decoding of hidden meanings, but by inventing different devices each time that aim to prevent the reader from perceiving the truth. And while her work experiments with many forms of blindness, it stages the proof of that blindness by its opposite, the unblinding that is the result of the police investigation—the interpretation and action by which *meaning is produced*.

It is this wealth of the modalities of blindness and of the production of meaning that motivates our work here, taking literature and what it has to offer as our point of departure.[1] For the real psychoanalytic use of literature, detective or otherwise, is not simply to reveal some latent mysterious content but also, through the variety and complexity of its models, to allow us to reflect on psychic phenomena and the conditions for understanding them.

All theoretical literature on the detective mystery genre is dominated by a principle of disguise that Agatha Christie seems to have perfected, a principle summarized in two rules.

The first is that the truth must be hidden throughout the book. The detective novel has meaning only if the truth is not revealed until the end of the book, and, if possible, not until the last few pages. This game-playing dimension is essential to the construction of blindness, which is all the more powerful when the veil is lifted at the last possible moment.

The second rule of the disguise principle: While being hidden, this truth must be accessible to the reader, even in plain view. It would would be out of keeping with the genre for the truth to be connected to elements unavailable to the reader, such as an unknown character, a hidden clue, or the like. This second rule distinguishes this type of novel from other detective stories in which the main emphasis is less on solving a mystery than on describing a milieu or evoking an atmosphere.

This fundamental principle of the detective mystery was established most clearly by S. S. Van Dine in an article published in the September 1928 issue of the *American Magazine*[2] (a work that is of course contemporary with Agatha Christie's *The Murder of Roger Ackroyd*). In it, Van Dine (pseudonym of the American writer Willard H. Wright, creator of the character Philo Vance) tries to formalize what he considered the twenty rules of the detective genre.

The seventh rule—on which we shall not insist while still endorsing it—requires the minimal necessity of one corpse per book: "There simply must be a corpse in a detective novel, and the deader the corpse, the better. . . . Three hundred pages is far too much pother for a crime other than murder. After all, the reader's trouble and expenditure of energy must be rewarded."[3] Other rules, more original, concern the identity of the culprit. Thus, according to Van Dine, it could never be a policeman or a detective ("This is bald trickery, on a par with offering someone a bright penny for a five-dollar gold piece"[4]) or a servant ("The culprit must be a decidedly worth-while person"[5]). He has to have played an important role in the story—he cannot be a marginal character appearing in the final pages—and he must be unique: "The entire indignation of the reader must be permitted to concentrate on a single black nature."[6]

But the chief rule, listed as number fifteen, concerns the method of concealing the truth:

> The truth of the problem must at all times be apparent— provided the reader is shrewd enough to see it. By this I mean that if the reader, after learning the explanation for the crime, should reread the book, he would see that the solution had, in a sense, been staring him in the face— that all clues really pointed to the culprit—and that, if he had been as clever as the detective, he could have solved the mystery himself without going on to the final chapter.[7]

Here we recognize the principle of the purloined letter. This principle of the truth hidden by its obviousness is most perfectly illustrated in a short story that has the twofold distinction of being one of the foundational texts of both detective literature and Lacanian psychoanalysis. In "The Purloined Letter" by Edgar Allan Poe, the story's thief has chosen an original way of concealing the document the police are searching for (a letter compromising the queen) by leaving it so plainly in view that the police take no notice of it.

We could read Agatha Christie's entire corpus as the rigorous and systematic application of the Van Dine principle. When we study her novels together, we realize that they involve experimenting in great detail with all the possible combinations allowing the application of this two-sided principle that prevents the reader from grasping the truth even while it is exposed in full view.

The first and the most classic way of making sure that the reader does not arrive at the truth is to *disguise* it, or to disguise one of its basic elements—to transform it in order to make it unrecognizable. This concealment can be applied, first of all, *to the murder itself*. No murder, no murderer. The murder will thus be disguised as a suicide (*The Moving Finger*) or as an accident (*Elephants Can Remember*). On the other hand, a natural death will be disguised as a murder (*Funerals Are Fatal*). More subtly, the cause of death may be invisible (*Towards Zero*). The disguise can also be a partial one and bear on that crucial element of the murder, namely, the time it was committed (*Death on the Nile, The Perilous Journeys of Hercule Poirot*).

More often, the disguise involves the murderer himself, since he is the crucial medium of the truth, at once the object and the subject of concealment. This disguise can apply, in the first instance, to his *nature*. In this case, a murderer's particular personal trait, whether physical (such as his age: in *Crooked House*, the murderer is a ten-year-old girl), relational (in *Hallowe'en Party*, it is a father who kills his child), or psychological (in most of the novels, the murderer tries to present a favorable self-image), dissuades the reader from thinking of him.

The murderer's *function*, in the sense of his professional activity, also has the value of protection, especially when it is an honorable one. Thus we encouter several physician murderers in Agatha Christie's work (*Cards on the Table, What Mrs. McGillicuddy Saw/4:50 from Paddington*), but also a pharmacist (*The Pale Horse*), policemen (*Hercule Poirot's Christmas, The Secret of Chimneys*), and a judge (*Ten Little Indians*).

Function protects even better when it is not simply a profession but is more subtly understood as a literary function, namely the narrative role. Two forms of this disguise are frequently encountered. A classic way of creating illusion in the detective novel is to *disguise the murderer as a victim*. Certain murderers try to convince others that they themselves are being persecuted or threatened with death (*Peril at End House, Death Comes at the End, Funerals Are Fatal, A Murder Is*

Announced). Also, this method of concealment often involves feigning death. This is the ruse to which the murderer resorts in *Ten Little Indians*, convincing his shipwrecked companions that he has died so that he can go about his murderous work undisturbed.

Another way of using the character's literary function, well known since *Oedipus Rex*, consists of *disguising the murderer as an investigator*.[8] Since he is on the side of the law, the murderer reaps the natural benefits of a kind of presumption of innocence. Apart from the case in which the murderer is himself a policeman (as in *Hercule Poirot's Christmas* or *The Secret of Chimneys*), this presumption of innocence is more broadly extended to all those who aid and abet the forces of order. This is the case in *The ABC Murders*, in which the murderer helps the investigators, or *The Man in the Brown Suit*, in which a high-level civil servant directs the inquiries against himself.

The last way of disguising the murderer is to *disguise him as absent* in order to make him invisible. This is the technique of the alibi, in which some material point indicates that he was not in a position to commit the crime, either because he was elsewhere (*Murder in Three Acts, A Pocketful of Rye, Murder at Hazelmoor*) or because, although present at the scene of the crime, he did not seem to have been physically in contact with his victim (*Murder with Mirrors*). This disguise as absence, which offers an alibi, often leads the murderer to disguise himself, this time in the usual meaning of the word, in order to return to the scene of the crime for a moment where he is determined not to be discovered (*Murder in Three Acts, Funerals Are Fatal, Murder with Mirrors*).[9]

The principle of disguise is to make any identification of the truth impossible. Faced with one or another of its telltale signs, the reader does not recognize it as such, because all forces are marshalled to prevent this identification from taking place. In the same move (distracting the reader's attention from such a sign makes it available for other purposes), the author will often strive to turn the reader's interest toward other clues. This time we are dealing with a kind of negative disguise. It is not that the truth is made unrecognizable, but that the false, we might say, is dressed up to draw attention to itself. We shall call this second mechanism of concealment *distraction*.[10]

Distraction can draw attention to other characters, who are rendered suspect solely to keep the reader's interest from settling on the character that matters. The most typical example of this is *The ABC Murders*, in which—throughout the book and parallel to the investigation—the reader follows the life of a character whose initials are those of the mysterious criminal signing himself ABC. This character behaves oddly and is, moreover, found staying in all the towns where a murder is committed.

Distraction can also involve clues. The reader's attention is then drawn to signs that mean nothing, either because they lead to a false solution or because they lead nowhere (in *Pocketful of Rye*, the murderer senselessly plants a cinder in one victim's nose and grains of rye in the pocket of another). If all the novels include false signs, the most remarkable of them figures in *The Clocks*. The murderer has placed four clocks near the corpse, all set forward in time. Hercule Poirot refuses to be drawn into this trap, having understood that these clocks are of no interest, their only function being to complicate the mystery.

Distraction can also be used as a plot device. In *The ABC Murders*, the reader is misled by a series of crimes attributed to a murderer who follows the alphabet. The reader thus forgets to concentrate on *each* individual crime and does not perceive that only one of these crimes interests the killer, who has committed the others only to distract attention. In *Murder in Three Acts*, the murderer commits three successive murders, only the second of which matters to him. He performs the first for training purposes (an actor by profession, his perfectionism

requires a general rehearsal) and the third in order to complicate the problem. The murderer in *Funerals Are Fatal* tries to
pass off a natural death as a poisoning. Attempting to steal a
Vermeer painting, he kills the owner of the picture, thought to
be the only one to have witnessed the first murder.

The advantage of distraction is that it highlights the aim of
detective fiction, which makes it unique among literary forms:
to prevent an idea from taking shape. Most literature tries to
stimulate a certain idea or a certain group of images or sensa-
tions in the reader, but here we find ourselves in that original
situation in which all the tension of the work is directed,
through a detailed organization of invisibility, toward *the pre-
vention of thought.*

Disguise and distraction work together, like two aspects of the
same movement whose goal is to keep the reader at a distance
from the truth. In these two strategies, which Agatha Christie
has inventively combined in numerous ways, the truth is concealed and is nowhere spelled out. If it were, the plot would
collapse immediately. Scattered through the text, the truth
emerges only when the reader has reassembled these fragments
that have been made deliberately unrecognizable.

Yet Agatha Christie resorts to a third, more original way of
concealing the solution: *exhibition.* This technique consists of
making the truth invisible by inscribing it in every letter. *The
murderer is, shall we say, hidden behind the murderer.*[11] This
is what happens in Agatha Christie's very first novel, *The Mysterious Affair at Styles.* Alfred Inglethorp, the man everyone
accuses—and later revealed as the guilty party—does everything in his power to incriminate himself. And Hercule Poirot,
who suspects him of poisoning his rich wife, does everything
possible to prevent his being charged with the crime.

The reason for this doubly peculiar attitude has to do with
an oddity of English law. A person who has been charged once
cannot be charged again with the same murder if the charge is

dismissed. So Alfred Inglethorp has prepared a very good alibi for the day of the murder. His plan is to produce this alibi when he is charged (and only then), so as never to be troubled again. Thus his method consists of placing himself in plain sight to protect himself.

This method of concealing a person is used in the same novel with an object. The day of the murder, Alfred Inglethorp writes a compromising letter to his accomplice, a letter in which he admits to the murder. Surprised by an unexpected visitor and at a loss for a place to hide the letter, he cuts it into thin strips which he places in a vase exhibited in plain sight on the mantlepiece. Here we recognize the principle of the purloined letter.

The same method is at work in another novel, *Towards Zero*. Nevile Strange, who has murdered his old aunt, concocts a whole series of particularly damning clues against himself, hoping the police will conclude that no such obliging murderer could possibly exist and turn their attention to a more discreet network of clues incriminating his former wife, Audrey. She is Nevile Strange's true target: he wants to take revenge on the woman who left him by having her accused of murder and sentenced to death. Similarly, the apparent murder, the killing of the old woman, conceals another—the only real one—that unfolds undetected before the reader's eyes: the murder of Audrey Strange, pushed slowly toward her death throughout the book.

An identical method is replayed in the short story "Witness for the Prosecution." Suspected of murdering a very rich old woman who has made him her heir, the protagonist Leonard Vole admits to his lawyer that he has only one alibi: His companion, Romaine Heilger, saw him return to the house before the time of the murder. But at the hearing, refusing to come to Vole's aid, Heilger explicitly accuses him and swears that, rather than returning at the stated time, Vole arrived later, covered with blood, and confessed to committing the murder.

Vole's case seems desperate when his lawyer receives an anonymous letter demanding an appointment. He meets with an old beggar-woman who offers to sell him a packet of letters. These were written by Romaine Heilger to a secret lover, and she confides in one of them that she has decided to get rid of Leonard Vole by having him falsely accused of murder. The reading of the letters at the hearing is devastating to the case, and although many incriminating elements remain, Leonard Vole is acquitted.

Observing at this moment that Romaine Heilger's gestures are remniscent of the old beggar-woman, the lawyer understands that they are the same person and that he has been duped. He goes to the young woman and asks her why she has played this charade, to which she answers:

Why did I play this charade? I was mad to save him and the testimony of a devoted woman would have been inadequate, as you yourself told me. However, I know the psychology of crowds. If my words at the hearing seemed to have been torn from me, they condemned me in the eyes of the law as a false witness, but the prisoner would immediately benefit from a favorable prejudice.[12]

And the story ends with this exchange between the lawyer and the young woman:

"I continue to believe," Maytherne declared with a puzzled air, "that we could have had Vole acquitted by normal means."

"I didn't dare take the risk. You assumed he was innocent."

"I understand," murmured Maytherne. "You were sure of it . . ."

"You were not," replied Romaine. "As for me, I knew . . . that he was guilty."[13]

This method is perhaps most perfectly embodied in *Murder After Hours*, in which the murderer allows himself to be apprehended near the corpse with a revolver in hand. This is not, in fact, the murder weapon, which he has hidden earlier, and ballistics analysis clears the suspect all the more easily since the police cannot believe that the real murderer would have voluntarily drawn attention to himself. A variant of this ploy figures in *Death on the Nile*, in which the murderer publicly announces in advance his desire to kill, then fires ostensibly at the future victim's companion, thus discrediting his responsibility for the murder in advance.[14] The same method can be extended to several characters. Both members of the murdering couple in *The Murder at the Vicarage*, for example, take great pains to incriminate themselves, so that the investigators think that each one is denouncing himself to protect the other.

In all these cases the method is the same: The concealment of the guilty party is achieved by exposing him. This method of *lying by means of the truth* recalls the joke cited by Freud in which a Jew, learning that another Jew is going to Cracow, scolds him for trying to make him believe that he is going to Lemberg in order to conceal that he is going to Cracow.[15] Faced with suspects as ostentatious as Alfred Inglethorp, Nevile Strange, or Leonard Vole, the reader is inclined to think that if the writer is introducing them with such ostentation, they must be innocent.

In these cases, in which the murderer is hidden behind the murderer and the truth behind the truth, the truth cannot be completely told or the book would make no sense: The name of the guilty party is announced by the text, but not the whole operative mechanism. Thus the suspect Nevile Strange is certainly revealed as the murderer, but only by his accomplishing the murder in an unexpected way, different from the one the investigators had in mind. These texts are equally prevented from telling *the whole* truth, since they are polyphonic and allow, at least until the investigator's final statement, a multitude of characters to express themselves. Because of this, erroneous versions of the story circulate in the reader's mind. In the end, we find ourselves face to face with a case that is different from disguise or distraction, in which the truth, to escape the reader, is not hidden but exposed.

These three major modes of concealing the truth are not mutually exclusive, and it often happens that a novel employs two or three simultaneously. We have seen that disguise and distraction are often used in tandem, that their conjunction facilitates the creation of illusion. Besides, it is rare that exhibition is not present, as least in some part of the book. If no turn of phrase suggests that a certain suspect is the murderer, our attention would inevitably be drawn to him.

One of these modes of concealment can also be doubled. This is the case with disguise, which always profits from being reinforced. So the murderer in *Ten Little Indians* is protected by his respected status, by his participation in the investigation, and by his function as victim. The killer of *The ABC Murders* resorts to a double distraction, of plot and suspect. "Witness for the Prosecution" rests on a multiple exhibition, since the whole set of conditions of the murder is exposed to the court by the murderer's accomplice.

The possibility of combining these three major modes of concealment, then, considerably augments the virtual number of solutions to a mystery by setting up a plural logic.[16] As a result, this diabolical inventiveness prompts us to wonder whether Agatha Christie's work is devoted to the means of concealing truth or to the difficulty of arresting meaning. The variety and complexity of the solutions proposed, while they ought to reinforce the Van Dine model by multiplying examples of its pertinence, rather progressively reveal its weak points. In the end, Christie's work generates a model of *polysemy* (a multiplicity of meanings) in which each indefinitely reversible element becomes subject to caution.

This multiplicity of meanings is, in the first instance, factual, since every novel, at least until the final plot resolution, explicitly proposes a whole series of readings. But it is also virtual to the extent that the probabilities we have just discussed in detail overarch the whole text like a reserve of hypotheses that are valid until the final resolution imposes one of them. This reserve seems nearly unlimited when we take into account the three major models of concealment already discussed and the possibilities of using them simultaneously.

The question is, then, *to what extent this virtual multiplicity of meanings finally generates undecidability*, therefore annulling the model of readability that Van Dine proposes. The chief drawback of this model—dominant in the theory and practice of the detective mystery—is its insistence that the reader's imagination must be struck, in the end, by a single solution. Yet there is no indication that the final solution exhausts all the possibilities offered by the combinatory play latent in the text, even while the work of Agatha Christie shows us its power of invention.

Doubt is even greater since blindness, as well as its dissipation, are personal phenomena. The idea of a truth placed in plain view, if understood objectively, is especially appropriate to novels based on exhibition, but it is much less so to those that resort to disguise or distraction, where the murderer sets up obstacles to perception. And the cases of exhibition that might illustrate this obvious fact offer a hypothesis of weakened reading, since the book continually challenges it. So the truth in plain view, whatever the mode of concealment, remains above all subjective and cannot be generalized: It is less a textual fact than a virtual reading, to which each person can assent or not. And the reader's gesture of assent, when it occurs, must not make us forget that assent might have been given to other readings, for our forgetting could well benefit particularly shrewd murderers seeking to escape scrutiny.

CHAPTER 4

THE LIE BY OMISSION

How is the reader—at least the reader who did not suspect Dr. Sheppard and accepts Poirot's proposed solution—fooled in *The Murder of Roger Ackroyd*? If we try to situate Agatha Christie's novel in the context of her whole corpus and in the framework of the major laws of illusion that we have formulated, a certain number of similarities and differences with the examples mentioned in the previous chapter become clear.

Conventional wisdom has it that the guilty party in this novel is not identified because he is hidden behind the narrator. But such a representation of the text is liable to lead us to oversimplify the way the deception operates. It is not, in fact, *one* isolated element, famous as it may be, that creates the illusion here, but a complex set of interlocking elements that call attention to distinct modes of concealment.

In many respects, the novel uses the method of *disguise*. Sheppard, whom the reader of necessity gets to know from the inside, does not seem endowed with a nature predisposed to murder. He is presented to us as a steady, even-tempered person with a solid sense of humor, capable of having some perspective on events.

The disguise by nature is matched with a disguise by function. Sheppard is a leading citizen in the village, where he practices medicine. Known and respected by everyone, he attracts less suspicion than a servant like Parker, a ne'er-do-well like Ralph Paton, a tramp like Charles Kent, or an adventurer like Hector Blunt.

Furthermore, he is intimately associated with Poirot's investigation. This function, as we have seen, is likely to fool the reader. This protection is even greater since Sheppard is continually associated with Hastings, a sterling character and Poirot's usual confidant—the very model of probity and candor—whose place the doctor takes temporarily.

Finally, and most importantly, Sheppard would be under greater suspicion were he not provided with a solid alibi: Several witnesses convincingly attest, having heard his voice, that Roger Ackroyd was still alive after the doctor's departure. The importance granted to the auditory deception in the book demonstrates that Agatha Christie did not have complete confidence in the method of hiding the murderer behind the narrator. Especially because of this alibi, the possibility of Sheppard's guilt does not occur to most readers, or if so, only fleetingly.

As often happens, disguise is associated with *distraction*. The reader's attention is regularly attracted to several suspects: in the first instance to Ralph Paton, and to a lesser degree to Parker and Charles Kent. Ralph Paton is the chief beneficiary of Ackroyd's large fortune, and he is on the grounds of the estate the evening of the murder. Parker is accused by Poirot of having blackmailed his former employer. Charles Kent is introducted as an aggressive social outcast addicted to drugs; one can easily imagine him committing a murder.

Several characters lie on minor points, promoting the reader's distrust: To hide the fact that she has stolen money from her uncle, Flora Ackroyd confirms that she met him after 9:30 P.M. Her mother, Mrs. Cecil Ackroyd, conceals the fact that shortly before the murder she entered her brother-in-law's study to check his will. The secretary Geoffrey Raymond does not acknowledge that he needs money and that the sum Ackroyd bequeaths him will be extremely useful.

Distraction also operates along the tangent of parallel intrigues, such as those uniting Ralph Paton with his wife, Ursula

Bourne, and Elizabeth Russell with her son, Charles Kent. Each of these intrigues, long kept secret, produces clues that distract the reader's attention: a wedding ring, a piece of torn apron, and the quill of a feather used for snorting cocaine.[1] Distraction is at work here since explaining these clues contributes nothing to the discovery of the truth, save to eliminate false leads.

Moreover, clues can be gratuitous, like the four clocks cited earlier. For instance, the police spend a good amount of time and energy trying to track down the fingerprints found on the murder weapon, until Poirot suggests the correct solution: The prints are those of the dead man, pressed on the dagger's handle by the murderer in order to complicate the investigation.

It is true, however, that a chief form of concealment here arises from the confusion of narrator and murderer, a murderer ostensibly placed before the reader's eyes throughout the book. Barthes says, correctly, that in *The Murder of Roger Ackroyd*, the reader seeks the murderer behind the "he" when he is really hidden behind the "I."[2]

Indeed, one of the specific features of *The Murder of Roger Ackroyd* is that it is written in the first person. While this narrative element certainly has a definite impact on the detective story, it is not so unusual. At least ten novels are narrated in the first person by Poirot's usual assistant, the faithful Captain Hastings. There are other examples of narrator-characters, such as the pastor in *The Murder at the Vicarage*, the nurse in *Murder in Mesopotamia*, or the convalescent patient in *The Moving Finger*. Still, this first-person act of stating is a major element in both the investigation and the narrative, for it means that all information in the book passes through the single prism of one subjective voice.

The act of stating as it is set up in this novel involves an ambiguity that Agatha Christie knew perfectly well how to manipulate. Since the book is a monologue, the first-person narrator merges, in the end, with the function of the omniscient narrator—on the model of the Balzacian narrator, that repository of all knowledge in the story, who organizes the progressive unfolding of many novels without appearing directly. Merged with this impersonal narrator, the "I" tends to become not simply one character among others but a mouthpiece for the truth.

In a sense, this particular place of the "I" makes him invisible to the reader while still in plain view. Hence the presumption of innocence that protects the figure of the narrator, at least in some novels. This presumption is, moreover, reinforced by the trust that is naturally given to the character who seems closest to the reader and is in continuous contact with him. So the reader does not realize that he is seeing the world exclusively through the eyes of a killer.

To come back to the categories proposed in the previous chapter, this confusion of the murderer and the narrator rests in the first instance on a form of disguise. Agatha Christie's cunning was to manage to *disguise the murderer in the process of narration* as that invisible and trustworthy voice which ostensibly discloses the story to the reader as if it were above suspicion because it is quasi-divine in origin—as if it were the utterly detached voice of the narrative itself.

The concealment of the murderer behind the narrating "I" would not work, however, if the narrator did not have recourse to two other closely connected methods that are essential to the production of illusion. The first is a technique of writing, and the second amounts to a narrative bias with much broader consequences.

The technique of writing is the use of *double-edged discourse*—statements that offer two possible but completely contrary, or at least distinctly different, readings. The use of double-edged discourse arises in some cases from Sheppard's taste for wordplay, but it emerges more pervasively throughout the book from a problem of narrative structure.

The single narrative voice allows the narrator, in effect, to recount the facts while communicating his feelings about them. More frequently, Agatha Christie's omniscient narrator recounts events but does not tell us about himself, and rarely if ever communicates the character's thoughts. In the case of Hastings, all the narrator's thoughts are revealed, but to no effect since Hastings is innocent and does not understand anything that is going on.[3] He is a transparant character, whose external gestures reflect his inner self. The case of Sheppard is different, since he can never express his real feelings, yet the form of the narration compels him to do so. Precisely because of this difficulty, he manages *to tell nothing but the truth*, thanks to the use of double-edged discourse.

A feature of this double-edged discourse figures in the final conversation between Sheppard and Ackroyd. Ackroyd has just told the doctor about the existence of a blackmailer, to Sheppard's dismay:

Suddenly before my eyes there arose the picture of Ralph Paton and Mrs. Ferrars side by side. Their heads so close together. I felt a momentary throb of anxiety. Supposing—Oh! but surely that was impossible. I remembered the frankness of Ralph's greeting that very afternoon. Absurd! (V, 44).

For the reader who does not suspect Sheppard of being the blackmailer, the anguish he expresses refers to the idea that Ralph Paton might be the criminal. In fact, this anguish refers to another possibility—terrifying to him—that Mrs. Ferrars might have confided in Ralph Paton before she died.

One of the chief reasons for double-edged discourse is the narrator's growing anxiety at the development of the situation and the progress of Poirot's investigation. Thus Sheppard often accurately reveals his innermost feelings to us and worries, for example, about his sister's and Flora Ackroyd's eagerness to apply for help to Poirot: "My dear Flora . . . are you quite sure it is the truth we want?" (VII, 75). His anxiety grows ever greater as Poirot proceeds with his inquiries:

> He was silent for a moment. It was as though he had laid a spell upon the room. I cannot try to describe the impression his words produced. There was something in the merciless analysis, and the ruthless power of vision which struck fear into both of us (XVII, 185).

But double-edged discourse has other motives as well, one of which is the use of internal irony. This emerges from the ambiguous formulations that will not take on their full meaning until we reread the book. For example, when Sheppard evokes the figure of Mrs. Ferrars: "When had I last seen her? Not for over a week. Her manner then had been normal enough considering—well considering everything" (II, 19). Or when he declares to his sister, who judges Ralph Paton to be innocent because of his good breeding: "I wanted to tell Caroline that large numbers of murderers have had nice manners, but the presence of Flora restrained me" (VII, 75).

Compared to the cases mentioned earlier, then, we can say that *here the truth is at once disguised and exhibited*, since every sentence of the book can be read in two different ways, depending on the final solution one decides to accept. There are no lies in Sheppard's narrative, but neither is there truth, since *we are dealing with two texts at once*. In this respect, and contrary to the traditional image of the detective novel, which is reputed to be written for the sake of a single reading, *The Murder of Roger Ackroyd* is a book that contains at least two books, explicitly composed for the sake of a rereading.[4]

The second method necessary to deceiving the reader is *the lie by omission*. It is true that Sheppard tells the truth and, thanks to his use of double-edged discourse, nothing but the truth, but he does not tell *the whole* truth. The truth—in any case, the name of the killer—is never actually spoken, as it can be in *The Mysterious Affair at Styles*, *Towards Zero*, or "Witness for the Prosecution." Sheppard is never suspected before Poirot's final accusation. If he were, even for a moment, the entire edifice of the book would collapse. In this light we can understand the safety net that the alibi of the dictaphone represents.

The lie by omission rests in the first instance on the narrative of the murder:

> Now Ackroyd is essentially pig-headed. The more you urge him to do a thing, the more determined he is not to do it. All my arguments were in vain.
>
> The letter had been brought in at twenty minutes to nine. It was just on ten minutes to nine when I left him, the letter still unread. I hesitated with my hand on the door handle, looking back and wondering if there was anything I had left undone. I could think of nothing. With a shake of the head I passed out and closed the door behind me (IV, 48).

Sheppard himself comments on this passage, which "recounts" the murder, in the final pages of his confession. After expressing his satisfaction ("I am rather pleased with myself as a writer" [XXVII, 254]), he cites the preceding lines before adding: "All true, you see. But suppose I had put a row of stars after the first sentence! Would somebody then have wondered what exactly happened in that blank ten minutes?"

Thus the murder would be located between the expression "twenty minutes to nine" and the beginning of the following sentence: "It was just on ten minutes to nine..." in the blank space that separates the period from the "It." Sheppard, moreover, has good grounds for suggesting that it would have been more honest to insert an ellipsis to indicate that his narrative is incomplete.

But doing this only once would not be enough to complete all the gaps in his narrative. Ellipses might be inserted between every two sentences, indeed within sentences as well. For if we pay attention to it, the lie by omission appears frequently in the book, and if Sheppard is the killer, he has necessarily practiced it many times.[5] We must assume, for instance, that he took the dagger in the following passage (the theft is performed between the sentence ending with "more closely" and the next, beginning with "I was"), while he is examining the curios inside the silver table:

> Wanting to examine one of the jade figures more closely, I lifted the lid. It slipped through my fingers and fell.
>
> At once, I recognized the sound I had heard. It was this same table lid being shut down gently and carefully. I repeated the action once or twice for my own satisfaction. Then I lifted the lid to scrutinize the contents more closely.
>
> I was still bending over the open silver table when Flora Ackroyd came into the room (IV, 37).

Similarly, we must imagine that in the following passage, Sheppard omits (somewhere between "I stepped out" and "the village church clock") telling us that he has left misleading footprints outside Ackroyd's study windows:

> Preceding me to the hall, Parker helped me on with my overcoat, and I stepped out into the night. The moon was overcast and everything seemed very dark and still. The village church clock chimed nine o'clock as I passed through the lodge gates. I turned to the left towards the village . . . (IV, 48).

But the lie by omission applies equally to Sheppard's relationship with Mrs. Ferrars, which he says nothing about when he mentions her suicide, to his memories (indeed his regrets) of the murder, or . . . to his practice of lying by omission, which he fails to indicate.

The lie by omission is therefore a major technique in the production of illusion in *The Murder of Roger Ackroyd*—perhaps the central one. It is even likely that ambiguous language is used only in cases when this technique is clearly impossible, when the reader might be surprised by the narrator's silence at certain points in the narrative, or by his discretion with regard to his feelings.

This form of lie delineates the fourth major technique of concealing the truth in the detective novel. Furthermore, it introduces something quite specific in relation to the other three. While these are meant to falsify the reader's perception of the literary reality (done most effectively by exhibition), the lie by omission conjures away certain elements of that reality by failing to communicate them to the reader. This is a strange narrative situation, however, since it amounts to making elements of a reality disappear that do not exist in the first place.

Of course there seems to be a limit to such a method, which is *what the text says*. Thus Sheppard does not give us all the information about the murder in the course of his narrative; but these missing pieces are communicated to us after the fact. It is hard to see how the reader might have access to secret elements of the work if these were not supplied somewhere along the line. The lie by omission, then, would be merely a malfunction in the communication of data, not the fruit of a deliberate concealment.[6] Sheppard would lie, but not the text, which would, in time, deliver the missing elements, and the reader's active participation in completing the novel would therefore be useless.

Unfortunately, such a vision of things suggests that a literary text is coherent and is not riddled with improbabilities of structure or fact. But there are massive improbabilities of this kind in Agatha Christie's novel, as we shall see, and they shatter the idea that with all the facts given on the final page, the text will come to a neat conclusion without the reader's participation.

We see how this opens a door that will be difficult to close. For if we acknowledge that the lie by omission exists, we shall now have to integrate it as a hypothesis into the reading of every book. Far from being characteristic only of Agatha Christie's novel,[7] it is part and parcel of the detective genre, which is structurally inclined to delay the communication of the truth as long as possible. But we may also wonder if this doesn't occur in any narrative, which can never claim to tell *everything*.

The major drawback of acknowledging the lie by omission is that it breaks the limited boundaries of literary works wide open. In effect, if ellipses can be added anywhere—including within sentences—then what we were reading until now as a finite and coherent whole is merely an incomplete portion drawn from a much vaster text, and we run the risk of setting no limit on reading and interpretation.

As we see, deception is not only produced by the conflation of the murderer with the narrator, but by means of a complex model that braids together several techniques of concealment while simultaneously opening up formidable problems of interpretation.

The lie by omission deals a fatal blow to the Van Dine principle by infinitely multiplying the number of virtual solutions. It ferrets out its weak point and turns it easily against itself. Being more a process than a state, it lives under the constant threat of a new destabilization. Once an established fact, Sheppard's guilt joins the work's previously established facts, which are likewise destined to evaporate. The question inevitably arises whether, in this book in which everyone lies, there is not someone even more effectively disguised than Dr. Sheppard.

PART II

COUNTERINVESTIGATION

CHAPTER 1

ENDLESS NIGHT

Several decades after *The Murder of Roger Ackroyd*, Agatha Christie wrote a book mysteriously entitled *Endless Night*. The title comes from a poem by William Blake that includes these lines:

> Every Night and Every Morn
> Some to Misery are born.
> Every Morn and Every Night
> Some are born to Sweet Delight,
> Some are born to Sweet Delight,
> Some are born to Endless Night.

The narrator of the novel is a young man by the name of Michael Rogers. The book, in which Blake's lines are quoted as an epigraph, begins like this:

In the end is my beginning. . . . That's a quotation I've often heard people say. It sounds all right—but what does it really mean?

Is there ever any particular spot where one can put one's finger and say, "It all began that day, at such a time and such a place, with such an incident"?

Did my story begin, perhaps, when I noticed the sale bill hanging on the wall of the George and Dragon announcing sale by auction of that valuable property "The Towers". . . (11).

This property actually bears the name "Gipsy's Acre," and in the region of England where the story unfolds, people say it is cursed. Having fallen in love with the place, Michael Rogers would like to become its owner, particularly because one of his friends, Santonix, a brilliant architect, is prepared to build him a magnificent house on this site.

But Michael Rogers has no money. Having gone from one chance profession to another over the years, he is hardly in a position to buy "Gipsy's Acre," let alone indulge in a house built by Santonix. Everything changes with the second noteworthy event in his life: his meeting with Ellie.

In spite of his desperate financial situation, Michael Rogers attends the auction of "Gipsy's Acre," which, this time, finds no taker. After the gathering, he goes for a stroll on his dream property:

> My feet took me without my really noticing where I was going along the road between the trees and up, up to the curving road between the trees to the moorlands. And so I came to the spot in the road where I first saw Ellie. As I said, she was standing just by a tall fir tree and she had the look, if I can so explain it, of someone who hadn't been there a moment before but had just materialized, as it were, out of a tree. She was wearing a sort of dark green tweed, and her hair was the soft brown color of an autumn leaf, and there was something a bit insubstantial about her. I saw her and I stopped. She was looking at me, her lips just parted, looking slightly startled. I suppose I looked startled, too. I wanted to say something and I didn't quite know what to say. Then I said,
> "Sorry. I—I didn't mean to startle you. I didn't know there was anyone here" (IV, 35).

The conversation becomes animated and the two young people are drawn to one another. Gradually, they both start dreaming, half jokingly, about "Gipsy's Acre" and the house that might be built there. The atmosphere is somewhat dampened when they meet an eccentric old woman who predicts a dire future for them if they persist in their attachment to "Gipsy's Acre."

In the weeks that follow, Michael and Ellie see each other regularly in London. He quickly comes to understand that Ellie is immensely rich. He then learns that "Gipsy's Acre" was sold to a mysterious buyer, who turns out to be the young woman herself. Set on marrying the young man with whom she has fallen in love, she has decided to engage Santonix to build Michael's dream house.

In spite of opposition from Ellie's family, who see Michael as a fortune hunter, the marriage takes place. Santonix builds them a magnificent mansion and the young couple settle in, despite the old woman's repeated warnings. Nothing mars their happiness except the growing influence of Ellie's best friend, Greta, a young German woman living on the property, who keeps Ellie under her thumb and for whom Michael feels an increasing aversion.

Several months pass. One morning, Michael goes into the neighboring town to attend an auction while his wife is off horseback riding. Worried when Ellie does not keep their luncheon date, Michael goes to look for her and discovers her dead, the victim of a heart attack suffered during her ride.

His wife's brutal death leaves Michael in possession of a colossal fortune. He travels to the United States to attend her funeral services and settle his inheritance, then returns to Europe by ship to "Gipsy's Acre." We are now in the penultimate chapter of the book:

Yes, that was what I was doing. It was all over now. The last of the fight, the last of the struggle. The last phase of the journey.

It seemed so long ago to the time of my restless youth.

The days of "I want, I want." But it wasn't long. Less than a year . . .

I went over it all—lying there in my bunk and thinking.

Meeting Ellie—our times in Regent's Park—our marriage in the registrar's office. The house—Santonix building it—the house completed. Mine, all mine. I was me—me—me as I wanted to be—as I'd always wanted to be. I'd got everything I'd wanted, and I was going home to it (XXIII, 216).

If the formula "I'd got everything I'd wanted" is ambiguous, this is not the case several passages later:

I came up on deck as we were approaching England. I looked out as the land came nearer. I thought, "I wish Santonix was with me." I did wish it. I wished he could know how everything was all coming true—everything I'd planned—everything I'd thought—everything I'd wanted (XXIII, 217).

Readers who have not guessed it discover that throughout the book they have been witness to a sophisticated murder that can be traced by a long look back at the text. Begin with a couple of lovers, Michael and Greta. She is the governess and best friend of a rich heiress, Ellie, over whom she has a considerable influence. So she proposes that her lover marry Ellie, then murder her. In order to accomplish this, Greta arranges for the two young people to meet at "Gipsy's Acre." Then she uses all her influence over Ellie to persuade her to marry Michael. The two criminals—who only pretend to hate each other to conceal their complicity—put cyanide in the capsules the young woman takes each morning for her allergies. Her death seems all the more natural since they have led Ellie's family and friends to believe that she has a heart condition.

The eccentric old woman, paid off by the criminals, is hired to lend a supernatural touch.

While *The Murder of Roger Ackroyd* involves only several ambiguous statements, here the entire book is written in falsified language. A primary reason for this deception is that Michael Rogers is a much more obvious suspect than Dr. Sheppard. Not only is he an adventurer and no respected citizen, but he is the direct beneficiary of Ellie's death, which leaves him in possession of a huge fortune. The disguise of person—with respect to professional attributes or narrative function—therefore does not work. For this reason, Agatha Christie has been careful to pass off the murder as an accident—resorting to the disguise of the murder—and to show that Michael Rogers could not have been present at the scene of the crime.

Double-edged discourse becomes even more important here as preparation for the murder takes place over nearly a year. Therefore a multitude of events can be recounted in a way that completely skews the reader's perspective and conceals their true sense.

Reread in this light, the key scenes in the book take on a different meaning, beginning with the encounter scene with Ellie: "And so I came to the spot in the road where I first saw Ellie." The reader may well feel that this is the scene of a first encounter. Yet we might say that *it both is and is not* a scene of a first encounter. It is certainly the first time that Michael actually *sees* the young woman, and in this respect his dazzled and surprised description is not deceitful. But it is also a false first encounter, since the young woman has been carefully prepared and manipulated by the two accomplices.[1] The whole book is constructed in this way, as Agatha Christie multiplies formal inventions in order to incite the reader *to read and not to read* each of the decisive sentences.

This is true of the day when the murder takes place as well.

Extending to an entire chapter the method Sheppard has already used, Agatha Christie lends the narrator a whole series of equivocal formulas. Thus Michael Rogers makes several repeated allusions to his happiness: " 'A wonderful day,' I said to myself with conviction. 'This is going to be a wonderful day.' I meant it. I was like those people in advertisements that offer to go anywhere and do anything. I went over plans in my head . . ." Or farther on: "I just woke up feeling happy this morning. You know those days when everything in the world seems right" (XVII, 166). These sentiments, which precede the discovery of the murder, arise not from the happiness of a man in love with his wife but from the satisfaction of thinking that she is about to die. . . .

More subtly, in the same chapter, the narrator never expresses a moment's concern at not seeing his wife at their luncheon date. But this is difficult to see at first reading, since we are predisposed to project anguish into sentences that in no way express it. So the narrator has the following conversation with his friend Major Phillpot while sitting at the restaurant table and waiting for Ellie, who fails to show up:

> "I wonder if she's forgotten all about it," I said suddenly.
> "Perhaps you'd better ring up."
> "Yes, I think I'd better."
> I went out to the phone and rang. Mrs. Carson, the cook, answered (XVII, 172).

Contrary to what the reader may think at first reading, what Michael wonders about is not that his wife may have forgotten to come. He is in a position to know that this is not the reason for her absence. The real meaning of "I wonder"—but this meaning emerges only upon rereading—is whether it is more prudent in front of a witness to confirm all hypotheses.

An identical principle is used a few lines later, at the end of the telephone conversation:

I told her I was at the George at Bartington and gave her the number. She was to ring up the moment Ellie came in or she had news of her. Then I went back to join Phillpot. He saw from my face at once that something was wrong.

The virtuosity with which Agatha Christie employs double-edged discourse throughout the book should not hide the fact that it is not, contrary to appearances, the major tool of deception. Once again, as in *The Murder of Roger Ackroyd*, it is the lie by omission.

This mode of falsification is indeed present everywhere in the book. The reader is not informed about Michael and Greta's history as lovers—the primary of its two love relationships—and whole swaths of their existence, such as their stay in Germany, are completely missing. Omission plays as much of a role in the organization of Michael and Ellie's first encounter as it does in the narrative of the murder, since discussion of its preparation and implementation is omitted.

Equally passed over in silence, by the same method, are most of Michael's feelings, which are conveyed to us in double-edged discourse only at moments in the text where their absence would be too obvious and the reader might be unduly surprised by a narrative without any trace of subjective response.

What becomes clear in this text, even more than in *The Murder of Roger Ackroyd*, is that the function of double-edged discourse is above all to disguise the gaps left by the lie of omission, especially at moments when it is impossible to make whole swaths of reality disappear completely without attracting the reader's attention. Thus, double-edged discourse is in the service of a larger strategy that consists, of course, of telling nothing but the truth, though not the whole truth—far from it.

Thus the reader is much less fooled by the conflation of the murderer and the narrator than by the generalized omissions.[2] He is not led into error by the ways that reality is presented to him—whether these have to do with the plot or the language expressing it—but by the fact that entire segments of this reality are stubbornly hidden from him until the final revelation.

The primary reason for the general ambiguity of language in *Endless Night* is that its referent, if not its subject, is *The Murder of Roger Ackroyd*. Having become famous with a novel whose murderer is the narrator, Agatha Christie could bring off this performance a second time, forty years later, only by making the method absolutely invisible, even to those whose aquaintance with the previous work might have made them suspicious of a narrative written in the first person by anyone other than the irreproachable Hastings.

So the Van Dine principle is carried to its extreme here. Not only is the truth, as always, exhibited in plain view, but it was even written once before, in another book that met with considerable success. So the real secret message of the book is less Michael Rogers' guilt than Agatha Christie's capacity, in full view of every experienced reader, to perform her sleight of hand once more.[3]

CHAPTER 2

THE PARADOX OF THE LIAR

Another original aspect of *Endless Night*, when compared to *The Murder of Roger Ackroyd*, concerns its ending. Returning to England after his wife's burial, Michael Rogers is approaching "Gipsy's Acre" where his beloved Greta is waiting for him. All of a sudden, rounding the bend, he sees . . . Ellie, looking straight at him. Terrified by the apparition, the young man reaches the house where he finds Greta waiting to celebrate their shared victory, but she does not manage to revive his spirits. Having lost his mind, he kills her in a fit of madness. The last chapter, written in hallucinatory fashion, clarifies the status of the entire book. It is a confession, written at the demand of the investigators, who have finally unmasked the murderer.[1]

The end of the book casts doubt on the entire telling. The fact that the narrator is a liar and a criminal is already damaging to his credibility. But if he is mad, too, and subject to hallucinations, the whole story is marked by a high degree of undecidability. This is especially true since the final revelation is not attributed to a capable and articulate investigator, as it is in *The Murder of Roger Ackroyd*, but to the murderer himself, who admits his guilt while haunted by phantoms.

The end of the book, moreover, makes the writing quite improbable. If it is a confession made at the request of the investigators, why draft whole passages so that they might be read in two distinct ways? Our general impression upon re-reading the book—especially of the way the narrator lingers over certain episodes— is rather of a man (Rogers) who has fallen into his own trap, a man sincerely in love when he thought he was only pretending.

We are struck, for example, with the thought that the scene
of love at first sight may not conceal a marriage scam but,
indeed, a scene of love at first sight.

> My feet took me without my really noticing where I was
> going along the road between the trees and up, up to the
> curving road that led between the trees to the moorlands.
>   And so I came to the spot in the road where I first saw
> Ellie. As I said, she was standing just by a tall fir tree and
> she had the look, if I can so explain it, of someone who
> hadn't been there a moment before but had just materi-
> alized, as it were, out of the tree. She was wearing a sort
> of dark green tweed, and her hair was the soft brown
> color of an autumn leaf, and there was something a bit
> insubstantial about her. I saw her and I stopped. She was
> looking at me, her lips just parted, looking slightly
> startled. I suppose I looked startled, too. I wanted to say
> something and I didn't quite know what to say. Then I
> said,
>   "Sorry. I—I didn't mean to startle you. I didn't know
> there was anyone here."

How can we avoid sensing a lover's emotion here, in the way
the young woman is so warmly described when the narrator
recollects their first hours together? And why not go even further and wonder whether Michael is really the murderer,
whether there isn't someone who is pulling the strings and
making him take responsibility for the murder, in this book in
which he seems to be manipulated by his accomplice?

Endless Night is interesting because it comes close to display-
ing a caricatured version of a problem already present more
discreetly in *The Murder of Roger Ackroyd*. This problem has
to do with the narrative structure of these novels written in the
first person and the undecidability this inevitably promotes. In

the third-person novel, the omniscient narrator guarantees the veracity of the story, at least theoretically, while in the first-person novel, the narrator is one character among others (Agatha Christie's considerable cunning depends on the idea that the reader does not regard him as just another character), and even his confessions must be considered suspect. *The first-person narrative does not tell a story; rather, it offers a point of view on a story.*

The fact that the narrator is a liar only underscores the original fragility of the act of stating. If he is presented as a liar, there is no more reason to believe him when he talks about the murder than when he does not talk about it, especially if he is mad. In other words, what makes these Agatha Christie novels so strong as narratives is just what makes them questionable as detective novels. The reader is most often fooled because he forgets that the narrator is also a character, therefore a possible liar, and therefore a possible murderer. But even if he is a liar, he need not be a murderer. The "I" is naturally the bearer of suspicion—not only to the detriment of the accused but also to his advantage.

Here we locate the chief contradiction of *The Murder of Roger Ackroyd*, which, to this point, appears never to have been pointed out before. The final pages of the book, taken together, amount to holding the narrator responsible for the statement, "I am a liar." If he does not express himself explicitly in terms of the ancient paradox, he acknowledges it implicitly as his act of stating is progressively destabilized. Moreover, he comes quite close to it at the end of his narrative, when he writes: "I am rather pleased with myself as a writer" (XXVII, 254).

In fact, it is Epimenides' paradox—and not a buried truth—that lies at the heart of *The Murder of Roger Ackroyd* and its reading. In its long version, the paradox reads, "Epimenides the Cretan says 'All Cretans are liars,'" and in its shortened version, "I am lying." We know that this paradox is an old logical conundrum and usually considered insoluble. In effect, if I say that I am a liar, my statement cancels itself out and I am telling the truth. But by saying it, I am therefore a liar, and my statement cancels itself out, and so on.

As Lacan has shown,[2] this paradox is not insoluble, provided we take the trouble to distinguish the subject of the statement from the subject of the act of stating. "I am lying" is pronounced both as the statement and as the act of stating, and the pronoun "I" condenses two subjects so that one disappears behind the other. The "I" who pronounces the formula differs from the "I" of "I am lying." One is in a position to tell the truth even as the other is declared a liar.

But this purely logical solution to the paradox does not solve the detective problem, which depends not on the analysis of levels of language but on the credibility of testimony. If Dr. Sheppard is a liar, if the act of stating is unreliable, then all of the book's statements must be considered suspect and not, as Hercule Poirot urges, only a limited number of them.

Although works like *The Murder of Roger Ackroyd*, and especially *Endless Night*, highlight a narrative contradiction in the detective novel, we must remember that this contradiction is not confined to novels told by a murderer, a liar, or a madman; they simply make it more obvious.

All mystery fiction in effect implies the narrator's bad faith. The genre dictates that even when this narrator is not the murderer or even a character but simply the vaguely embodied act of stating, his job, for most of the book, is to lead the reader astray. Not only does the narrator refrain from telling everything he knows, but by a highly selective presentation of the facts—the series of decoys we analyzed above—he ensures that the reader will be led off in the wrong direction.[3]

Since the narrator, even if he knows the truth, is tainted with bad faith, how credible is the solution that he finally endorses—whether alone or through the intermediary of a detective? The paradox of the liar is particularly glaring when the narrator is a murderer, but it is no less present in every narrative form whose aesthetic brief is to produce mistaken illusion.

It is the connection between representation and writing that is operating here. Trying not to represent an imaginary reality—as in most fictional literature—but to trick the reader by presenting a skewed version of this imaginary reality, the detective thriller produces an insoluble contradiction that undermines all veracity and makes the final solution it tries to impose suspect.

This contradiction is all the more apparent in Agatha Christie's novel, which poses a general problem of construction that doubles the structural question of the act of stating. Unlike other novels by the same author written in the first person, such as *The Murder at the Vicarage, Death on the Nile* or *The Moving Finger, The Murder of Roger Ackroyd*, though consisting exclusively of Sheppard's narrative, is not a homogeneous text but is composed of two extremely unequal parts. The first begins with the death of Mrs. Ferrars and includes the first twenty chapters.[4] The second is Sheppard's final confession, consisting mostly of the last chapter entitled "Apologia."

Between these two texts we find in succession the public gathering of suspects organized by Poirot and the private conversation with Sheppard, which ends in an accusation of murder. At the end of this interview, Poirot asks Sheppard to finish his manuscript by putting an end to his lies by omission: "But Captain Ralph Paton must be cleared—*ça va sans dire*. I should suggest that you finish that very interesting manuscript of yours—but abandoning your former reticence" (XXVI, 252). So Sheppard takes one night to write a little more than six chapters, which seems physically possible.

Yet these two texts—whatever their actual boundaries—are as contradictory in content as they are in tone. The first text presents us with an irreproachable narrator, akin to the pastor in *The Murder at the Vicarage*; the second tends increasingly to accuse him. The calm and distanced account gradually gives way to an anguished tale. Certainly the second part of the book, although appreciably shorter, is meant to cancel out the first. But since the two parts are attributed to the same character, there is no reason not to entertain the hypothesis that the first part might in reality be more truthful.

Confronted by these two texts, the reader can decide to choose the second, in conformity with the classic detective model, in which the truth is progressively revealed in the interpretive movement that dissipates all false leads. But he may well wonder whether the "truer" text might not be the first. And this would prompt him to try and discover what event could have induced Sheppard to start lying.[5]

Similarly, Sheppard admits nothing. Because of this, the second part of the book contradicts itself in a way.

As we have seen, his reactions to Poirot's accusations are expressed as compassion. After accusing the detective of being mad, the doctor scolds him for having brooded over this case too long, then admits that he does not know where this will lead. Finally, Sheppard observes that—as every reader of Agatha Christie knows—Poirot is not short on suggestions, and thanks him for "a most interesting and instructive" evening. At no moment in Poirot's presence does he make the slightest gesture toward confession.

On the other hand, the final chapter, which announces Sheppard's suicide, seems more explicit, at least on first reading. If he does not explicitly confess the murder,[6] several passages unquestionably designate him as the murderer. The first concerns the murder weapon:

The dagger was an afterthought. I'd brought up a very handy little weapon of my own, but when I saw the dagger lying in the silver table, it occurred to me at once how much better it would be to use a weapon that couldn't be traced to me (XXVIII, 253).

It is an accusatory passage, intensified by these words:

I suppose I must have meant to murder him all along. As soon as I heard of Mrs. Ferrars's death, I felt convinced that she would have told him everything before she died (XVIII, 253-254).

But under close scrutiny, neither of these passages implicates him explicitly. Others seem more accusatory, like those that deal with the dictaphone, and we shall examine these in greater detail in the context of our solution. They lead, however, to no direct form of confession. What is clear—in any case if he is now telling the truth—is that Sheppard had *intended* to kill Roger Ackroyd. But it is not clear that he did it. So we find another omission that balances the major omission of the murder itself: the absence of a confession in the confessional chapter.

These final pages are dominated rather by a juxtaposition of ambiguous statements, composing a text that can be effectively read as an acceptance of the detective's conclusions. But they might just as easily be read as an incitement—intercut with a few ironic gestures of compliance—to the reader not to allow himself to be overcome by Poirot's interpretive euphoria and for the reader to pursue the investigation himself.

Even if Sheppard were to confess, his confession would prove nothing. The police are quite familiar with such mythomaniacs. In all democratic forms of justice, the confession of a presumed culprit is only one element of the indictment, nothing more. The real issue is: Was he physically in a position to commit the murder? And, as we shall see, nothing is less certain.

CHAPTER 3

IMPROBABILITIES

Apart from the general structure of the book, which is a machine for producing the undecidable, Poirot's solution, when we examine it more closely, reveals a fair number of improbabilities. Pronounced too quickly in a state of misleading euphoria, it hardly resolves the many problems raised by the investigation.

Provided the novel is read carefully, it contains such a great number of improbabilities that, for the clarity of exposition, we will group them into three categories: those that concern the hours preceding the murder; those that involve the act of murder itself; and those that concern the period following the murder.

To investigate the period before the murder is to investigate the *motive*. Moreover, Sheppard clearly poses the question to Poirot: "What on earth had I to gain by murdering Ackroyd?" (XXVI, 250), to which Poirot replies in these words:

> "Safety. It was you who blackmailed Mrs. Ferrars. Who could have had a better knowledge of what killed Mr. Ferrars than the doctor who was attending him? . . . If Ackroyd had learnt the truth he would have had no mercy on you—you were ruined for ever."

Let us consider, for a moment, that Sheppard may indeed be the blackmailer.[1] Just how would his safety have been threatened, and, following the hypothesis that it were, how would the murder dispel this threat? If he is guilty, Sheppard is not taking much of a risk. A blackmailer does not use checks, and transfers of funds cannot be traced.

Moreover, the epistolary confidences of a murderess—Mrs. Ferrars, in her letter of accusation, owns up to her husband's murder—who is dead besides, may be easily discredited. In the face of a letter of accusation, delivered posthumously, the most reasonable attitude is denial, attributing such accusations to amorous spite or any other motive, and putting the burden of proof on the investigators, who will find it very difficult in the absence of the victim.

But this is the case only *if* the murder solves the problem. *There is no guarantee that Mrs. Ferrars confined herself to a single letter* and did not send a second—to the police, for example. If a blackmailer's victim is determined to harm him, she may do more than simply denounce him to her lover— especially when she eliminates further risk by committing suicide. How could Sheppard have known that only one letter accusing him existed, and that Ackroyd's murder therefore made sense?

Which leads us to another problem aside from motive, namely, the psychology of the alleged murderer. There is a fundamental contradiction between the suggested portrait of a cold and calculating mysterious killer and that of a Sheppard going mad at the thought of a danger that is nonexistent (or at least that should be confirmed), at risk of imperiling his safety—this time for real—by committing a murder. These two images do not coincide.

More broadly, Sheppard, presented as a weak-willed fellow, hardly fits the occupational profile. These character traits are confirmed several times by his sister (XVII, 182), but also by other characters, notably Poirot (XVII, 183). Yet this weakness does not square with the decisive frame of mind the murderer must have had to kill Ackroyd only a few hours after the announcement of Mrs. Ferrars' death.

*   *   *

Improbabilities connected to the act of the murder itself are still greater, and rest for the most part on the fact that Sheppard has very little time at his disposal between the moment he learns of Mrs. Ferrars' death that morning and the time he is supposed to have killed Ackroyd that evening.

Concerned as he is with establishing to the minute how Sheppard occupies his time, Hercule Poirot does not seem to pay attention to a simple problem. Let us carefully review the doctor's activities on the day of the murder (chapters II–III). His morning is devoted to medical visits, then to seeing patients at his office. He lunches with his sister, and afterward goes into his garden to do some weeding. This is when he makes the acquaintance of his neighbor, Hercule Poirot, with whom he has a long conversation. At the end of this talk, he goes back into the house, where he has a new discussion with Caroline. After a certain time, on the pretext that he has a client to see, he goes off to the Three Boars Inn, where Ralph Paton is staying. The book communicates to us only the beginning of the conversation between the two men, and, after a gap in the account, we find Sheppard in front of the house at Fernly Park, a little before 7:30 P.M.

The text does not give us Sheppard's precise schedule, and we have to entertain several conjectures. Suppose that his lunch with his sister took place at around 1:00 P.M. and lasted an hour. The long conversation with Poirot might then have taken place between 2:00 and 3:00, the shorter talk with Caroline between 3:00 and 3:30 P.M., the meeting with Paton between 4:00 and 4:30 or 5:00. We would also have to add travel time between the Three Boars and Sheppard's house, and between the doctor's and Fernly Park.

Why are these precise details of schedule so important? Because the killing of Ackroyd, at least in Poirot's version, not only requires the possession of a weapon, it also implies the construction of a sophisticated device, namely a kind of programmed timer that Sheppard must invent and construct from scratch out of a dictaphone. The question that arises, then, is

When? The time for the conception and construction of this object is very brief since Sheppard learns only that morning that he might be in danger, and until then had nothing to worry about. But the time for manufacturing such a complex precision instrument is even briefer, since Sheppard has a maximum of two hours in a house where Caroline leaves him no respite, and where he has little hope of isolating himself to fabricate (this is 1926) what must have been the first clock-radio in technological history.

Ackroyd's murder does not depend only on the lightning-quick fabrication of a timing mechanism. It also depends on a pair of shoes, which Sheppard is supposed to have filched from Paton in order to leave misleading footprints.

Several improbabilities are connected to this enterprise. Paton, though merely passing through King's Abbot, has to have brought along several pairs of shoes, or he would have soon noticed the theft. How could Sheppard have been sure of this in advance? We later learn that he returned to the inn when Paton was gone in order to steal the shoes. This makes some sense, since clearly, it would not be so easy to steal a pair of shoes from a room at an inn *in their owner's presence.* Sheppard is then reputed to have brought them in his medical bag. This, too, is not completely impossible, even if we must imagine him armed with an enormous sack, since he is already carrying a weapon and a dictaphone in it besides! Finally, in Poirot's logic—for otherwise Sheppard would incriminate himself as the person who stole them—Sheppard has to return the shoes to the inn, where he again runs the risk of being noticed.

All this is extremely difficult to execute but not impossible. On the other hand, another point is entirely improbable. When Poirot, in a turn of phrase, casually mentions the shoes Sheppard must have stolen from Paton to fabricate false clues (XXV, 248), he tends to underestimate the difficulty of imitating someone's footprints. Indeed, we learn during the investigation that the weather had been dry, and it was thanks to a chance bit of damp gravel that the tracks had been identified (VIII, 94). Now, when Sheppard was plotting his murder, that is something he could not have foreseen.

Even more surprising than the dictaphone and shoe escapades is the telephone call, on which Poirot's solution hinges almost entirely. Let us recall that on his return from Roger Ackroyd's house on the evening of the murder, Sheppard receives a telephone call attributed to Parker, the butler, supposedly informing him of his master's death.

We concur with Poirot and see this as the key to the whole affair, but by interpreting it in a radically different way. As Poirot sees it, Sheppard wants to be sure he is at the scene of the crime when the body is discovered, and has asked one of his patients, a ship's steward leaving for America, to call him from the train station. He then tells his sister he has received this call from Parker and must go immediately to Fernly Park.

Far from incriminating Sheppard, the story of the telephone call tends to suggest his innocence if we apply a modicum of common sense. Even assuming that he needs to be at the scene of the crime at that moment, we may well wonder why he resorts to such a complicated and risky procedure, which is so dangerous and so useless as well. The complication is obvious. It is risky since Sheppard's entire strategy rests on the hope that the steward will not forget to call. The danger is amply demonstrated by what happens, namely, that the police easily manage to trace the call.

But most of all, the telephone call is perfectly useless, and this is why it suggests Sheppard's innocence. If he had wanted to be on the spot, he could easily have done what everyone (including characters in other Agatha Christie novels) does who wants to return to a place they have just left: pretend to have forgotten something, such as his valise or some other medical object needed for his visits the following day.[2] This is a simple, foolproof method that involves no external participation or any lie that the police might exploit.

This ruse would also have the advantage of resolving a problem that the solution imagined by Poirot leaves untouched: For Sheppard's presence at the crime scene to have any meaning, he needs to be left alone in the room to retrieve the dictaphone and slip it into his bag. He manages this by sending Parker, the only one awake, to inform the police. But the risk is great, in Poirot's version, that the other inhabitants of the house will wake up, informed of Ackroyd's death by the doctor's arrival.

Sheppard's attitude after the murder is not very clear. First of all, it is difficult to understand why he devotes so much energy to putting the police on the right track. After Ackroyd's demise, there is no longer anyone, by definition, who might know about the blackmail of Mrs. Ferrars. Yet *it is Sheppard himself who informs the police of this blackmail* and tells them about the blue envelope.[3]

Another cause for surprise is Sheppard's attitude toward Paton. As we know, the doctor spirits the young man away from the investigation by hiding him in a psychiatric hospital. This initiative can be explained if Sheppard is protecting the young man. It becomes more enigmatic if he is the murderer, and, curiously, Poirot does not raise this point during his accusation. Just how does concealing Ralph Paton help to disguise the truth? (We can see how effective it is when Poirot forces Paton from his refuge.) Save by killing him, too, Sheppard cannot hope to keep Paton sequestered forever. Once the young man is free, Sheppard's part in his concealment will necessarily come out.

Sheppard's attitude after Poirot's accusation is also quite odd. This man who is reputed to have killed in cold blood to protect himself does not even dream of denying Poirot's reconstruction, which nonetheless rests on extremely shaky ground and contains no real proof.[4] The small discrepancy in Sheppard's schedule, like the displacement of the highbacked chair, hardly merits much attention. More seriously, the telephone call may have a different explanation from Poirot's, as we shall see. Sheppard, however, offers no protest, thanks Poirot for the evening, and runs off to commit suicide. Strange behavior, requiring a few explanations.

This series of improbabilities does not lead us, we see, to proof positive of Sheppard's innocence or a declaration that he could not possibly participate in the murder. But Poirot's accusation leaves a number of gray areas. It cannot be excluded that Sheppard is the killer, but it is also possible that he is not. In any case, a jury would be unlikely to condemn him on such flimsy evidence, with so many elements unexplained and no attempt to clarify the remaining murky facts. All indicators make it desirable, then, to reopen the investigation.

CHAPTER 4

THE IDEAL MURDERER

Who then? The first possible answer to the question *Who killed Roger Ackroyd?* is the logical consequence of the book's structure, of the way the illusion is constructed according to the Van Dine principle. This answer illustrates to what extent the detective thriller depends on an original semiological mechanism that is likely to invite reflection on the meaning and conditions of its production. Moreover, it can be transposed to most detective novels of this kind, to the extent that this problem of structure is reciprocally related to their own organization and their concerted practice of falsification.

The detective thriller does not function as a seamless whole but works in two successive movements. The first of these, which lasts for most of the book, is a movement of *opening meaning* and tends to multiply leads and solutions. Without exploring all combinatory possibilities—far from it—this movement develops explicit proposals as well as more discreet suggestions, conjuring before the reader's eyes for brief moments a multitude of possible worlds in which different murderers commit virtual murders.

The second movement, which intervenes at the end of the book, is a movement of *foreclosing meaning*. It brutally eliminates different possibilities and privileges a single one, charged—in conformity with the Van Dine principle—with clarifying all proposed mysteries in retrospect while giving the reader the feeling that it was there in front of him all the time, protected by his blindness.

Now, these two movements are essentially contradictory,

since one tends to enlarge possibilities, the other to limit them. The second movement, which proposes a unique textual truth, certainly attempts to cancel the multiple meanings organized up to this point by substituting a single meaning presented as necessary after the fact. But so many hypotheses are generated by the combination of different possible decoys that the movement of foreclosure runs a serious risk of leaving a certain number intact.[1]

This problem is even more important since, as we have seen with regard to the novels of Agatha Christie, there are several modes of concealment, and their combination generates a wide-open space of virtualities. To take only one example, the technique of exhibition insures that several of the solutions proposed by the text—which the reader would be tempted to reject as too obvious—can, according to certain readings, be considered quite valid after the fact, precisely because of their obviousness. So we are justified in wondering—as with our book—whether certain characters, far from being exonerated, shouldn't be considered suspect simply *because* they are suspects.

This difficulty of foreclosing meaning is inherent in the peculiar logic of the detective sign, or *the clue*. As it opens, the narration disseminates a considerable number of clues, only a few of which have any meaning by the end of the book. Among the multitude of clues produced by the investigation, Hercule Poirot retains only a small number: a five-minute discrepancy in the narrator's account of his whereabouts, the displacement of the highbacked chair, and the telephone call supposedly announcing Ackroyd's death. And he neglects many others— some of which shall be the basis of our own reading—either because he does not perceive them, because he considers them irrelevant, because he understands they are merely dead ends, or because he explains them by showing that they are not directly connected to the murder.

Indeed, Agatha Christie's detective novels display the difficulty of interpretation at work, which is in the first instance *the difficulty of deciding what to interpret*. For *everything* can be interpreted in a text (physical traces, behavior, words), especially if this text has been constructed in such a way as to both disseminate and obscure meaning. For this reason, interpretation seems to rely upon a preliminary major operation of *selection*, which determines the boundaries within which interpretation can be exercised.

But this preliminary difficulty is immediately matched by another, which has to do with the *comprehension* of signs. The proliferation of false leads increases the number of readings, since every sign, once suspected of generating meaning, can supply the point of departure for several different readings. Such is the case with the traces left by Paton's shoes or the telephone call to Dr. Sheppard, which will probably be clues in *all* readings, but will not carry the same meanings.

What seems clear, then, is that the clue is less a sign already present than a sign *that is constituted after the fact in the movement of interpretation*, which, by proposing a definitive meaning, ranks the givens and builds a plausible textual structure backwards. In this way, the clue does not so much predate the interpretation as become its product.[2] This after-the-fact aspect means that the same signs—or the same meanings of the same signs—will not be mobilized in every reading, which is another way of saying that with each reader mapping his own network of clues, *everyone is not reading the same text*.

Agatha Christie's work clearly exposes the plural nature of the clue and its infinitely malleable character. This multiplicity of meaning produces a kaleidoscopic image of the literary text, which can be reconstructed in various ways, depending on the ultimate solution. Reversing any attempts to promote the Van Dine principle, this polyphony of meanings is put into play, even if the final pages reduce it artificially to something unequivocal by insisting that it is possible to fix its meaning definitively in a text that has at last become the same for everyone.

It is certainly logical that the author's solution, or what passes as such, should take precedence, but it is rare that it suffices to destroy all leads—and therefore all possible texts—especially when the narrative is in the first person and that person's credibility is in question. If the end of the book determines what is a clue and what is not, it does not always manage to reabsorb all the signs, or clues, that have been previously disseminated. Thus other reorganizations of the text based on other signs or other readings of the same signs, generating a different story every time, continue to have a virtual existence.[3]

Anxious to turn the reader's attention away from the truth at any price, Agatha Christie naturally allows us to attach our suspicions to suspects who have not committed the murder. Once the truth appears to be revealed, these other suspects are still not exonerated of all the charges against them. Take Ralph Paton, for example. To hold ourselves strictly to the logic of detective fiction, he is and he remains the most likely murderer. The charges remaining against him (everything in the text points to him) are not negligible, and are easily equal to those that allow Hercule Poirot to accuse Dr. Sheppard.

First, Ralph Paton has something Sheppard singularly lacks: a motive. He stands to inherit Ackroyd's considerable fortune, and this inheritance is all the more welcome as he is short of money. In addition, his secret marriage to Ursula Bourne has most likely poisoned his relations with Ackroyd, and so the formal cause is doubled by an immediate one.

Another element must be taken into account: the general psychology of the character. An unstable, attractive fellow with no professional life or social standing, Ralph Paton strongly resembles Michael Rogers in *Endless Night*, who is another version of Paton written forty years later. In this respect, too, Paton has what Sheppard does not: a murderer's profile.

While to have been present at the scene of the crime is not to have committed it, it is still surprising that Ralph Paton should have been there on the night of the murder, precisely at the moment that it was committed. He readily acknowledges that he was walking in the woods at the fatal hour and has no alibi.[4] To believe he is innocent is to bet on improbability against good sense.

Nor is it so banal to think that he might have left traces of his footprints behind. By stubbornly insisting that the prints traced to Ralph Paton's shoes were not made by their owner, Poirot eliminates the most logical hypothesis in favor of the bizarre scenario we have already reviewed, in which Sheppard was obliged to steal Paton's shoes from under his nose, then pray for a seepage of water under Ackroyd's window that very evening.

Clearly, in a hypothesis of Paton's guilt, the fantastic invention of the dictaphone with a delaying timer becomes useless and disappears.[5] The voice of the man who, according to several auditory witnesses, was speaking with Ackroyd just before his murder would be Paton's, making it all the more likely that Ackroyd, according to auditory witnesses, was indeed refusing to lend someone money.

The hypothesis of Ralph Paton's guilt does not explain everything, and leaves several aspects of Dr. Sheppard's puzzling behavior in need of clarification: the telephone call, the concealment of the suspect (Paton), and the doctor's attitude after Poirot's accusations. In any case, we are not claiming that Sheppard's attitude is logical or perfectly clear. But we are challenging the deduction by which these improbabilities or these lies would automatically make him the murderer, just as Poirot has unearthed similar lies and improbabilities among the other suspects without charging them with murder.

What Poirot refuses to consider is a simple hypothesis suggested by everything in the book: namely, Sheppard's constant concern to protect his good friend Paton, for whom he has paternal feelings. Curiously, one of Agatha Christie's novels, *Ten Little Indians*, is built entirely on this principle. In this book, Hercule Poirot is enlisted to investigate a murder committed fifteen years earlier by the daughter of the convicted woman, who has died in prison. He discovers that the mother allowed herself to be falsely accused of murder in order to protect the girl, whom she believed to be guilty.[6]

If we accept the hypothesis that Sheppard is protecting Paton for some reason, his attitude toward Poirot's accusations becomes understandable, especially his puzzling reluctance to exonerate himself. The same is true for his suicide and for the ambiguous wording of his final narrative. Similarly, concealing Paton now makes more sense than it does if Sheppard is guilty. Convinced that Paton is the killer, Sheppard is determined to keep him away from the law and secretly hidden in an asylum until he is able to escape abroad.

Obviously, all that remains is the telephone call—a stumbling block to any solution. The question is not who made the call—it can only be the steward—but why Sheppard uses this pretext to return to Ackroyd's house. Or, more precisely, assuming that he returns to eliminate traces of the murder, how can he be certain that Ackroyd is dead?

It is difficult to answer this question, first because the book does not provide the answer, but also because it offers a confusing number of choices. From Sheppard's account, he has clearly sensed throughout the day that a drama is about to unfold, and he goes to Paton's to try and avert it. We can imagine that his fear was reinforced when he met up with the young man on leaving the estate.

But there are many other possibilities, and a very simple one concerns the telephone call. We shall propose the hypothesis that Sheppard has guessed what happened, not because he received a telephone call but because he *did not*. It is unthinkable that after reading the name of the blackmailer, Ackroyd would not have called Sheppard (whether he had promised to do so or not). So by a kind of metonymy, or process of association, that would make Ackroyd's silence signify his death, Sheppard's announcement to his sister ceases to be a lie. The fact that after an hour the telephone rings only once, with a banal message, indicates that the drama may in fact have been played out, and that Roger Ackroyd may have been murdered.

Even after conducting his own investigation, Poirot is forced to recognize that all evidence points to Ralph Paton. There is only one solution that will exonerate him: "The real criminal must confess" (XXIV, 241). But, as we have seen, it is difficult to take Sheppard's ambiguous last words as a confession. By seeking a brilliant and complicated solution at any price, Poirot forgets that everything still conspires at the end of the book to make Paton, in the absence of an indisputable culprit, the most likely killer.

PART III

DELUSION

CHAPTER 1

CROSSROADS

Odd as it is, our proposal for rereading has at least one precedent, involving the most famous crime story in literature, the origin of both the detective novel and psychoanalysis: *Oedipus Rex*. In a letter to Wilhelm Fliess dated 15 October 1897, Freud cites Sophocles' play in order to advance his hypothesis of the famous complex. The play is said to prove Oedipus' guilt by recounting how, after a lengthy investigation, he arrives at the conclusion that he is his father's murderer and his mother's lover. But is this version of events beyond dispute?

On the face of it, the business of Laius' murder is a simple matter. Let's review the facts. In the wake of a mysterious epidemic that decimates the population of Thebes, King Oedipus, spouse of Jocasta, consults the oracle at Delphi, which announces that for the plague to end, the murderer of Laius, the former king, must be found. Oedipus then pronounces a curse against the murderer. He interrogates the divine Tiresias, who dodges the question to which he knows the answer, leading Oedipus to suspect him of committing the murder along with Jocasta's brother, Creon.

Jocasta then challenges Tiresias' clairvoyance, using as her example the prediction he made concerning her own son, suspected of one day becoming his father's killer. But Laius dies at a crossroads, killed by brigands. At the mention of a crossroads, Oedipus is overcome by anguish and hastens to return from the country to interrogate a servant who has witnessed Laius' death. This servant is the man charged with getting rid of Oedipus at his birth.

Just then a messenger arrives from Corinth, informing Oedipus of the death of Polybos, the man he believes to be his father. Since Oedipus is still worried about the possibility of marrying his mother, the Corinthian envoy reassures him by telling him that he was a foundling, and that Polybos was not his real father. Thus Oedipus is caught in the trap of fatality. Jocasta hangs herself, and Oedipus, enacting his own curse, blinds himself and leaves Thebes for exile.

Sophocles' play is a significant source for psychoanalysis, since Freud relies on this work—taken as reference, if not proof—to elaborate its major structure. Although Freud does not dwell on the Greek tragedy—but rather on another, equally foundational detective drama, *Hamlet*—*Oedipus Rex* nonetheless inspires the formation of the central complex of psychoanalysis by giving it both its emblematic name and its dramatic form.

Curiously, Sophocles' play is also the source of the detective novel, since it is the first literary text clearly constructed as such,[1] well before the formal constitution of the genre in the nineteenth century. All the elements of the detective novel are present: a murder, a killer, an investigator and an investigation, which serves as the framework of the story. It even contains the narrative twist that will later lead to numerous variations in which the killer—disguised by his function—is merged with the investigator.

Sophocles' play has been passed down to posterity as the model of tragedy—and as the model of the psychoanalytic cure, a stage version of painful introspection. But the commentaries have eclipsed its character as a detective story. Once recognized, however, this character opens the way to certain questions, some of which concern Freud's reading of the play, others the play itself, and still others its place as the inaugural example in psychoanalytic theory.

* * *

The first problem concerns Sophocles' play itself. Its detective structure inevitably invites highly detailed if not overly fastidious readings. Several authors since Freud have challenged the traditional reading.

A first approach to this challenge is formulated by Marie Balmary, in *L'Homme aux statues*.[2] The author of this work takes Freud to task for privileging only one of the Greek literary works dealing with Oedipus, Sophocles' play, to the detriment of works on the subject by Aeschylus and Euripides, which Freud may not have known.

This emphasis on *Oedipus Rex* tends to *highlight the sins of the son, Oedipus, while forgetting the sins of the father, Laius*. Balmary reminds us that the curse which falls on the son issues from crimes perpetrated by the father. After losing his own father, King Labdacos, Laius seeks refuge with King Pelops. There he conceives a passion for the king's son, the young Chrysippus, whom he abducts, bringing on himself Pelops' curse and provoking Chrysippus' suicide.

Balmary observes that the entire story now appears in a different light. The source of Oedipus' tragedy is no longer blind fate but a sin committed by his father: the abduction of his host's son, the homosexual violation, and the boy's suicide. Accordingly, this first sin is doubled by two others. Laius violates the prohibition on fatherhood which the gods have pronounced in response to his crimes. And finally—a third sin— having fathered a son despite this prohibition, he withdraws his gift of life and exposes his son to death.

These three sins leave traces in Sophocles' play. Laius has seduced another man's son and pushed him to suicide: His own son kills him, seduces his wife, and drives her to her death. He has not respected the prohibition on procreation: His people, victims of a mysterious epidemic, can no longer procreate and die. Finally, he has torn the tendons in his son's feet: The son destroys his own eyes. *Oedipus Rex* would be incomprehensible, then, without the imprints left by the crimes of Oedipus' father on its plot and even in the words of the play.

"Freud," observes Balmary, "did not see . . . that *Oedipus Rex* engages much larger questions than that of Oedipus' desires. And much more terrifying: nothing less than the transmission of original sin from generation to generation. The machine is inexorable: here, no pardon, no redemption; the evil done by the father will be expiated blindly by the son, who will transmit it once more to his own sons, until the extinction of his line" (38).

This first critique of Freud does not question Oedipus' guilt but tends to make it relative, situating it as the extension of his father's guilt. It is the message of the play or, if you will, Freud's reading, that is under discussion here. Those who challenge Oedipus' responsibility for the murder of Laius take a very different perspective.

Surely Voltaire was the first to express doubt about Oedipus' guilt, in a letter dated 1719:

Oedipus asks if there is anyone in Laius' entourage who can provide information; they answer him that "one of the men who accompanied that unfortunate king, being saved, came to tell in Thebes that Laius had been killed by robbers, who were not few but great in number."

How can it be that a witness to the death of Laius recounts that his master was overpowered by many men when it is yet true that it was a single man who killed Laius and his entire entourage? . . .

The Thebans would have had much more to complain about if the riddle of the Sphinx had not been easier to guess than all these contradictions.[3]

The problem of the number of Laius' assailants is unavoidable since Oedipus himself poses it in Sophocles' play. When he asks Jocasta to order the witness to the murder to return, Oedipus declares, "You said that he spoke of highway robbers who killed Laius. Now if he uses the same number it was not I who killed him. One man cannot be the same as many. But if he speaks of a man traveling alone, then clearly the burden of the guilt inclines towards me."[4]

To which Jocasta replies, "Be sure, at least, that this was how he told the story. He cannot unsay it now, for every one in the city heard it—not I alone."[5]

And Oedipus insists, "Right. But yet, send someone for the peasant to bring him here. Do not neglect it."[6]

"If we were in the genre of the detective novel," writes literary critic Sandor Goodhart in an airtight argument, "we would expect at this point that the witness would be summoned and interrogated about the matter for which he was summoned; as a result, the truth would be clarified. But . . . in the interval between the summoning of the witness and the witness's arrival, the Corinthian messenger has appeared and displaces the action toward the question of Oedipus' origin. . . . And it is this last subject exclusively that will be clarified by the shepherd's subsequent remarks. On the subject for which he was summoned, the subject on which the solution to the mystery of the play hinges, he is simply never interrogated."[7]

As Yale critic Shoshana Felman observes, after reviewing all the evidence in the case,[8] the investigation does establish that Oedipus is Laius' son, but certainly not that he is his murderer. Seeing the improbable prediction start to come true, Oedipus infers that it is about to come true altogether. Through a leap of logic he deduces his responsibility in the murder of Laius, but strictly speaking, and especially in terms of rigorous detective work, this remains to be demonstrated.

In her decisive article, Felman does not go so far as to attribute every consequence to the doubts that surround Oedipus' guilt, nor does she set out in search of the true criminal—the only way to exonerate Oedipus. She does not extend beyond her two chosen texts—*Oedipus Rex* and Sebastien Japarisot's *Piège pour Cendrillon*—a principle of undecidability that is clearly operating in these works. Yet this principle is also activated by the structure of every detective story. She does demonstrate, however, the underlying bonds that join the Freudian discovery of the unconscious to a literary genre based on the illusions of consciousness and the duplicity of all self-knowledge.[9]

Unlike Marie Balmary, whose criticism is directed explicitly against Freud, authors uncertain of Oedipus' criminal responsibility address themselves to the lack of rigor in Sophocles' play, which raises, but never resolves, the question of Laius' attackers.

It is true that if we accuse Sophocles' text of lacking rigor, we may be attaching a detective quandary to this text that is alien to it: In the logic of classical fatality, Oedipus is fated not to complete his investigation. Nonetheless, the contradictions are so blatant that they did not escape Voltaire an entire century before the birth of the detective genre.

Moreover, Freud's use of this text, and of *Hamlet*—a use based on suspicion—encourages this kind of reading. Unlike in Balmary's reading, its consequences for his work are only slight. It hardly matters whether we rely on a play in which there was no murder of the father to illustrate the Oedipus complex. For one thing, there is certainly incest. For another, and most importantly, Oedipus may accuse himself wrongly, yet Sophocles' play would indisputably remain shot through with *the fantasy of murdering the father*, which is more clearly located in this work than in the numerous literary texts that might be recruited to illustrate the Freudian complex.

It is more interesting to speculate to what degree Sophocles' play participates in the underground influence of a detective model on the founding of psychoanalysis. It cannot be mere coincidence that the three literary works that most influenced psychoanalytic theory—*Oedipus Rex*, *Hamlet*, and "The Purloined Letter"—are all detective stories. Moreover, other foundational works such as *Totem and Taboo* and *Moses and Monotheism*—stories of murder investigations—and to a lesser degree *Gradiva*, all depend on related schemas.

We are really dealing here with a model based on the Oedipus myth's twofold proposal linking the story of the Sphinx to the search for Laius' killer: The production of meaning should be related to the resolution of a mystery. This implicit assumption, evident in Freudian detective investigations, leads inevitably to *thinking of interpretation as a subsidiary of hermeneutics*, that major form of the production of meaning that continues to weigh heavily upon psychoanalysis and its system of representations.

It is not so much the prevalence of murder stories that matter in this literary model but a particular type of unambiguous signification which the detective mystery epitomizes. This signification is closely tied to a fixed form of investigation. The search for a killer as such is not as important as the search for the site of a truth beyond the complex traces of its concealment. A scrupulous investigation, based on a correct reading of the clues, would bring this truth to light.

Choosing the detective mystery as a model is a decisive choice in literature and art that privileges an aesthetic domain in which meaning is largely unambiguous. Solving a murder implies, if not the identification of a murderer, at least the existence of a stable truth that antedates the reader's encounter with the work. Moreover, it is taken for granted that the detective novel is rarely reread, at least while we still remember its ultimate solution and the way that solution curtailed the pleasure of puzzling out the mystery.

The detective model discourages a second reading because along with the clue, it imposes a dual conception of the sign, which is situated to produce a single meaning: that latent truth concealed by overt signs which the investigation finally brings to light. So the whole polysemic value of literature—its multiplicity of meaning—is made relative. Yet this value is inherent in the complexity of its forms as well as in the subjective intrusions of the reader, whose presence and speech create an unprecedented system of meaning.

Freud's recourse to the detective story as a model leads him to neglect both the reader as subject and the reading's aftermath. Given its unequivocal character, the solution to the mystery tends to make the interpreter's place relative—until this book, at least—since it antedates his intervention, prompting him to *find* rather than to *create*. He is left with the element of subjectivity and language that prescribes listening for what is inscribed, not inventing what is yet to come.

CHAPTER 2

WHAT IS A DELUSION?

As indicated in the introduction, it is impossible to resolve the question of the murder of Roger Ackroyd without posing the question of delusion, since these are counterparts. This book's entire effort, in fact, comes down to asking whether Hercule Poirot's solution, despite its seductive power, or perhaps because of it, is not utterly delusional.[1]

Unfortunately, despite the number of works devoted to delusion, it seems difficult to define the term with any precision, and this difficulty arouses a certain anxiety. In fact, the term is also used among psychoanalysts to qualify palpably different clinical realities. So it is not clear that the same label applies to the reveries of Norbert Hanold, the protagonist of Jensen's *Gradiva*, to the very organized constructs of Freud's famous patient Dr. Schreber, and to the disordered productions of schizophrenics.

For this reason, although we are initially concerned with the whole spectrum of delusional phenomena so as to define its scope and complexity, we will focus here on a particular type of delusion that might be confused with normal discourse. If at certain moments in his investigation Hercule Poirot is the victim of madness, it is surely this type of pathology.

A first element that should allow us to characterize delusion is *its falsified relation to reality*. Or, put more simply, the delusional person—Poirot, for example, in wrongly accusing Sheppard—does not perceive things as they are.

This falsification of reality is at the center of the delusional experience, whatever form it takes. Freud has shown that psychosis, the privileged domain of delusion, differentiates itself from neurosis by the changes it tries to impose in the perception of reality. The psychotic substitutes a more acceptable neoreality for an unbearable reality, whereas the neurotic is inclined to repress it in the unconscious.[2]

This first criterion, while it has the merit of pointing us in the right direction, is unfortunately very imprecise. Its formulation includes at least two problematic terms: *reality* and *falsified*. We can certainly imagine cases in which the reality would be unquestionable—this goes for murders or for unanimously acknowledged facts, like certain historical facts—but much of the time what is being falsified is itself in doubt.

A first example is the case in which the falsifiable reality pertains to the metaphysical, the privileged domain in which delusion flourishes. Thus it is customary to consider the beliefs of Dr. Schreber pathological. Yet they are not so far removed from certain religious dogmas that are not considered troubling, since the world to which they apply, the world of last things, is inherently inaccessible to verification.

Beyond the metaphysical sphere, delusion often focuses on human relationships, a realm in which the perception of rifts is largely personal and even constitutes an important part of these relationships. Witness the first-class delusion of jealousy: Even when a person is suspected unjustly, jealousy sometimes has a basis in an authentic if unconscious infidelity.

If the notion of reality is not very clear, the same is true of falsification. A certain behavior that we view as delusional impresses us, in fact, as a transformation of "reality," but it is unlikely that any untransformed relations with reality exist, even in the most "normal" person. Certainly this is a matter of degree, but such an answer hardly helps us to judge when it becomes appropriate to speak of delusion.

Although indispensable, this first criterion of identification is quickly revealed to be inadequate, especially since it does not allow us, for example, to distinguish between a delusion and a lie. Now, I can find myself producing perfectly incorrect statements that do not conform in the slightest to reality, without falling into the category of "delusional."

It seems a second criterion is needed to allow us to speak of delusion: *the feeling of conviction on the part of the person producing it.* This is the distinction between a delusion and a lie, a joke, or simply false information. If I spread the word that the Civil War is a completely fictitious historical event, it is delusional only to the extent that I truly *believe* this when every means of making the necessary verifications is available. In other cases, and depending on the circumstances, we might be dealing with deliberate disinformation, a hoax, or . . .

In our approach to the phenomenon, then, it might be appropriate to make a distinction between the statement and the act of stating. Delusion implies a major distortion of reality but at the same time a certain psychological position in relation to this distortion—a particular mode of engagement in discourse, and belief, or the radical absence of doubt, in the truthfulness of one's productions. Poirot sums this up very well in his third-person formula: "Hercule Poirot knows."[3]

This conviction is such that the author of the delusion sometimes manages to extend its reach by persuading others to share it. Indeed, one of its features is that it is not strictly an autonomous formula but may, in some cases, become a shared experience through the feeling of certainty it arouses in its listeners.

Although the feeling of conviction seems to be a criterion that is easily identified, it does pose another problem of evaluation. Everything depends on the psychic level at which this conviction is judged. Now, conviction that is confirmed—most often consciously—does not necessarily correspond to real unconscious conviction. The same person who confirms a statement halfheartedly can nonetheless be deeply persuaded of its rightness, sometimes without having access to this depth of conviction.

As imperfect as they are, these first two criteria are necessary to the identification of delusion. It is hard to label a discourse delusional when its author does not believe in it, whether it conforms to reality or not. Venturing the hypothesis that Poirot's theory is delusional, we encounter this distortion of reality in him (we offer the hypothesis that Sheppard is inno-cent) and the contagious force of a deep conviction (Poirot is clearly convinced of the justice of his thesis and is prepared to persuade the police to share it).

But we see immediately that these two excessively broad criteria are not always adequate, even in the case of Poirot. They would lead us, for example, to confuse delusion with error. I can sustain absolutely false ideas for a long period of time and with the greatest conviction (again, in relation to a clear-cut reality) without meriting the label delusional, which implies the presence of a whole pathological background.

Unfortunately, these two criteria also tend to imply that delusions are homogeneous and to ignore what may be essen-tial differences between them. So it is appropriate, here, to return to a rather classical psychiatric distinction between two large affective groups, *disorganized paranoid delusion*, or schizophrenic delusion, and *paranoid thought disorder*.

The first, which gives a large place to unconscious primary processes, seems to be unorganized, incoherent, and disjointed. There are few problems identifying this kind of delusion, since the subject is clearly in a strange and confused state. As such, this delusion is of little interest to us, since its recognition—at least on a phenomenological level—is easy, and clearly Her-cule Poirot is not affected by it.

On the other hand, paranoid thought disorder is more dif-ficult to spot, and that is what makes it both dangerous and interesting. Depending more than paranoid delusion or schizophrenia on secondary processes, it offers all the seductions of a reasoned discourse. Sometimes such a delusion is developed with great rigor, or so it seems, and presents itself to the observer as relatively plausible, even convincing. It rests on a logic difficult to fault, close to traditional logic, yet stiffened by a kind of detectable rigidity.

In fact, the logical processes at work here are carried along by an inner tension that stretches it to the limits of reason.[4] They are subtly motivated less by the necessity of describing or understanding the facts than by the ultimate solution that the author of the delusion has posed as preliminary (for example: Sheppard is the murderer). This solution bends all new information to its will and leads to dismissing all other ways of connecting the facts that a different solution would produce.

Hercule Poirot's final speech is a revelation of the apparently flawless but subtly biased logic that is at the heart of a paranoid thought disorder. All the facts described in his implacable demonstration seem linked according to acceptable relations of causality (which can convince his listeners) but are entirely dependent on the solution they are enlisted to serve. This *false coherence*—formidable because it challenges the boundary between normality and madness—is the third characteristic of this kind of delusion. At the same time it is what makes any identification so difficult.

This logic depends on a practice that is rarely absent in this form of pathology, namely, *interpretation*. Even if some delusions are more specifically called delusions of interpretation, interpretation is rarely lacking, whatever the structure of the emotion (jealousy, erotomania, megalomania) and its dominant themes.

The importance of interpretation is easily explained if we consider that delusional activity amounts to substituting a new reality for the existing one, rather than repressing it. In this view, interpretation is the enactment of this substitution, which transforms a dear friend into a traitor, or an odd occurence into a sign from God. The delusional person lives in search of a reality situated beyond appearances, one that interpretation, gradually revealing its secret outline, allows him to enter.

The primary place of interpretation gives great importance to the clue. As the imperceptible sign of the existence of this other reality, the clue is at the heart of delusional thinking; in it, the delusional person sees both the confirmation of his intuition and proof of his chosenness.[5] And it is significant that the clue is something shared by paranoid delusion and the police investigation, which are not so different in this respect.

Poirot's psychic behavior, which determines the dynamic of his investigation, illustrates this practice of interpretation and its attendant dangers. The clinician's suspicions are aroused by the way he obsessively focuses on minute signs—like a time difference of five minutes in Sheppard's schedule or the slight displacement of a piece of furniture in Ackroyd's study—while neglecting essential facts, as we shall see.[6]

His attitude is revealing in the way it excludes all significant data that have no direct bearing on his construction and threaten its coherence. This attitude demonstrates to what extent *the clue, even before it is an object of meaning, is a process of exclusion.* By attracting attention to itself, it subtly obscures all other clues that do not conform to the interpretive project and so cannot reach the threshold of critical perception.

The central place assigned to interpretation once again complicates the problem of identifying delusion. Following this view, a clinical reading is no longer limited to the observation of the phenomenon in question but becomes one of its basic elements. So the process of locating the phenomenon threatens to implicate the observer in what he observes. Since delusion is an overinterpretation, to qualify a discourse as delusional is to run the risk of becoming delusional oneself through an excess of interpretation. Even more than its other features, this nodal point of interpretation, while casting doubt on every reading, places delusion at the shifting encounter of subjectivities.

* * *

A last characteristic of delusion does not fall under the rubric of a descriptive phenomenology but of a Freudian watchword. Delusion is an *unconscious formation*.

To say this suggests that it should be thought of as a dream, a fantasy, or a slip, or even something like a literary work rather than as a simple thought disorder or isolated accident of language. Even if it seems mad in its psychotic forms, a delusion has an underlying meaning that is accessible to the intelligence if we take the trouble to discover what is at stake on the stage of the unconscious.

The psychoanalytic conception of delusion influences both its comprehensibility and its reach. Far from being a moment of incomprehensible madness, delusion, in this Freudian approach, can yield to interpretation. So we are led to think that Hercule Poirot's construction, should it be revealed as delusional, obeys an internal logic that ought to be made explicit because this logic makes it psychically necessary.

But this notion runs the danger of being extended and the identification of delusion made more difficult. If delusion is not as crazy as it seems, what we would be tempted to call delusional may be only the visible part of more common thought patterns. This would explain the anxiety raised by such psychic productions.

Despite the accumulation of criteria, delusion is not, therefore, a clearly delimited formation, and its identification involves a certain ambiguity. We can, of course, take heart by telling ourselves that the problems of demarcation concern the group of paranoias in particular, and within this group certain highly organized constructs; a completely mad paranoid fantasy will always be recognized. But a coherent delusion—the most interesting of all in the way that it mirrors normal thought— may be difficult to designate with any certainty.

Moreover, our five criteria underscore the illusion of objectivity in this arena. One of the difficulties of identifying delusion involves the part played by subjectivity implicit in this identification, since the subject who does the identifying cannot extricate himself from the discussion. Without going so far as to say that we are less delusional to ourselves than to others, this nonetheless seems to be true, especially in the case of an interpretive delusion such as the one to which Hercule Poirot may be victim, as its evaluation depends to some degree on personal feeling.

CHAPTER 3

DELUSION AND THEORY

The difficulty in discerning the boundaries of delusion arouses such anxiety that everyone feels legitimately threatened with becoming its unwitting victim. But this anxiety is still greater for the theoretician when he begins to wonder if there aren't too many connections between delusional activity and his own activity of research—if, beyond accidental similarities and subjective quandaries, there may not be a common structure. This is a more dramatic hypothesis than our first, which chiefly involved the character of Poirot. Such a supposition leads us to imagine the impossible situation in which no objective position on madness would exist any longer, the very context of this position having become conflated with its subject.

The apparently odd idea that connections between delusion and theory may exist seems to be one that preoccupied Freud throughout his work. On several occasions, in fact, whether implicitly or explicitly, he observes that the separation between the two discursive formations is far from clear. Above all, he suggests that the question is even more vital when it comes to psychoanalytic theory.

There are many texts relating to theoretical activity in Freud's work, and these take various forms. He is led to compare, somewhat disrespectfully, theory-making to fiction. Moreover, his regular attacks on philosophy can be interpreted as criticisms of a form of abstract thought disconnected from the real and akin, in this regard, to the rigor of a paranoid thought disorder.[1] It seems, then, that he perceives some theoretical activity as virtually pathological.

But on other occasions Freud goes a step further and suggests that theory itself may be, if not delusional, at least a form
of thought that contains some delusion. The most surprising
text on this point figures at the end of his commentary on the
Memoirs of Dr. Schreber. Freud begins by warning his readers
that the observations he is about to make may damage his
theory of libido in the eyes of many readers. Then he goes on
to compare Schreber's theory with his own:

> Schreber's "rays of God," which are made up of a con-
> densation of the sun's rays, of nerve-fibers, and of sper-
> matozoa, are in reality nothing else than a concrete
> representation and external projection of libidinal
> cathexes; and they thus lend his delusions a striking simi-
> larity with our theory. His belief that the world must
> come to an end because his ego was attracting all the rays
> to itself, his anxious concern at a later period, during the
> process of reconstruction, lest God should sever his ray-
> connection with him—these and many other details of
> Schreber's delusional formation sound almost like endo-
> psychic perceptions of the processes whose existence I
> have assumed in these pages as the basis of our explana-
> tion of paranoia. I can nevertheless call a friend and
> fellow-specialist to witness that I had developed my
> theory of paranoia before I became acquainted with the
> contents of Schreber's book. It remains for the future to
> decide *whether there is more delusion in my theory than
> I should like to admit, or whether there is more truth in
> Schreber's delusion than other people are as yet prepared
> to believe* [italics author's].[2]

The passage begins rather blandly with the observation of a
correspondence between Schreber's delusion and Freud's
theory. But this statement of a correspondence leads to a discussion of precedence—suggesting that Freud is defending
himself against the charge of plagiarizing Schreber—a discus-

sion that empowers the magistrate by making him part of the scientific community. It is hardly surprising, in this context in which the line between reason and unreason is no longer respected, that the paragraph ends with a sentence inextricably mingling madness and theoretical truth by attempting to clarify the part played by each.

The point of this text on Schreber is to show that if theory is threatened by delusion ("if there is more delusion in my theory than I should like to admit"), conversely, delusion presents affinities with the truth sought by theory ("or whether there is more truth in Schreber's delusion"). Despite the apparent symmetry between the two parts of the sentence, there is a virtual leap here, for madness shifts from the side of *deviance* to the side of *structure*. To say that theory is in part delusional is, in fact, less serious than to perceive the truth at the very heart of madness, which runs the danger of granting madness a fixed place in the process of theorizing.

Now, several of Freud's texts seem to point clearly in this direction. One of them is found at the end of his reading of *Gradiva*. This is no bland remark, since the hero of Jensen's story is a young archaeologist with whom Freud can easily identify. Pondering the conviction of those who suffer from delusion, he declares:

Now, however, it is time to ask if the course of delusion-formation which we have inferred from our author's representation is one known from other instances or one even possible. From our medical experience, we can answer only that it is surely the right way, perhaps the only one, in which delusion attains the unshakable acceptance which is part of its clinical character. If the patient believes so firmly in his delusion, this does not happen because of an inversion of his powers of judgment and does not proceed from what is erroneous in the delusion.

Rather, *in every delusion there is also a little grain of truth* [italics author's]; there is something in it which really deserves belief, and this is the source of the conviction of the patient, who is to this extent justified.[3]

Here again we find the indestructible conviction ("if the patient believes so firmly in his delusion") that is one of the decisive elements of delusion. But a new thesis is added that tends to legitimate this conviction: *The delusional person is, at least in some small part, on to the truth,* and as such deserves to be believed. This is a paradoxical formulation (truth and delusion are usually perceived as antithetical), but one that is not unique in Freud's work.

In a somewhat later text on infantile sexual theories, Freud returns to the truthful aspect of delusional theories: "These false sexual theories, which I will now describe, all have one very curious characteristic. Although they go astray in a grotesque way, yet they all, *each one of them, contain a bit of the real truth* [italics author's], so that they are analogous to those adult attempts at solution, which we call flashes of genius, of the problems of the universe that are too difficult for human comprehension."[4]

Here the question is not delusion, properly speaking, but allied formations, namely those false theories that children elaborate when they are faced with insoluble problems, such as where babies come from. The other term of the analogy concerns the solutions that adults find to problems which surpass human understanding, such as metaphysical questions. Again, truth is oddly situated at the heart of falsehood, as if, far from being its antithesis, it were its core or center.

Parallel to these texts, which contest the boundary between delusion and truth, another paper radically challenges the practice of construction. Freud, more relativistic than ever—seeming even to doubt the validity of his construct—gives himself over in these terms to a surprising comparison between theorizing and delusion: "The delusions of patients appear to

me to be the equivalents of the constructions we build up in the
course of an analytic treatment—attempts at explanation and
cure, though it is true that these, under the conditions of a
psychosis, can do no more than replace the fragment of reality
that is being repudiated in the present by another fragment
that had already been repudiated in the remote past."[5]

This time it is the very heart of psychoanalytic activity,
construction—or, if you will, the psychic act of theorizing—
that is called upon to account for psychotic delusion. More
particularly, it is the act of thinking by which the psychotic
substitutes a more acceptable fragment of reality for an unbearable one. Just as the analyst's intervention is assimilated to
a form of suggestion, madness, far from being cast as the opposite or the risk of theory, or even as strictly separate from it,
seems once again to offer something mysteriously "equivalent"
to it.

Attempting to put these disparate texts together, we see that
they reinforce the idea—implicit in the extension of our proposal in the previous chapter—that the boundary between
delusion and theory is unclear. This lack of clear boundaries is
expressed in a double assertion. First, theoretical constructions, at least psychoanalytic ones, involve something delusional. Second, delusion offers affinities (or an analogy or
equivalence) to theoretical activity.

These two assertions might be connected by using one of the
examples cited concerning infantile sexual theories. These
theories demonstrate to what degree the activity of theorizing
(that is, attempting to make meaning, to organize scattered
facts) is actually part of psychic work, not so much an object
of random application as the way the mind relates to the
world. Theory and delusion are all the more easily interwoven,
then, because they have a common source and a common base.

This interweaving may seem shocking, but it is explained if
we recall that in the Freudian view, delusion is less a form of

madness than its opposite, that is, *an attempt to put order in madness*. To initiate a delusion in the midst of a psychopathological process is an attempt to dispose of certain fragments of psychic life differently, to engage in the work of making meaning and therefore in a form of theorizing. This way of thinking of delusion even allows us to separate it from madness to some extent and view it, against the grain, as an attempted cure.[6]

The moment we view delusion from this angle, *as an activity of making meaning and not as a loss of meaning*, we see that delusion and theory are not radically opposed but rather both depend on a similar attitude of thought. This attitude finds its archaic origins in the subject's initial questioning and gives rise to various psychic productions—productions that are valued very differently on the cultural level but which are, at times, likely to present certain similarities.

In view of what infantile theories teach us, we might even wonder to what extent both the constitution of the "I" and its existence fundamentally depend on an activity of theorizing. In this view, theorizing would not be simply one occupation among others, or a period of sublimation, but an unceasing effort of psychic adaptation to internal and external threats— indeed, its very essence.

The place of the subject in theory is posed more clearly in delusion than it is in other psychic experiences. The question of the subject might be formulated in these terms: To what extent is a theory determined by the person who invents it or makes it his own?

As soon as we make the activity of theorizing internal to the subject, as Freud seems to encourage us to do, the boundary between theory and delusion is completely subverted. Just as a movement of theorizing structures every delusion, a certain portion of delusion similarly organizes every theoretical effort. Since this portion is characteristically baffling to others, it is tempting to ascribe it to the subject, to see it as belonging specifically to him and therefore defining him. While attempting to construct a meaningful story, then, he differentiates himself from others to the point of appearing, in their view, completely irrational.

To locate textually this subjective portion, or the psychotic portion of thought, is a risky business. First, it does not usually involve specific segments of theory but rather a much deeper movement by which the subject, from childhood on, questions the world and its origins. In addition, we can assume that identifying this subjective portion in theory is itself subjective, and therefore open to variations.

As arbitrary as this identification may be, we must not underestimate the importance of Freud's texts comparing delusion and theory and the way they displace a more traditional philosophical conception of the activity of thought. First of all, this activity is no longer seen as having only an independent relationship to the world or to truth, but as also having a relationship of psychic continuity with the subject who engages in it. And how we evaluate it is based less on a *truth* in itself, fixed and independent, than on a form of *truthfulness* to be measured principally in terms of the subject.

The acceptance of this idea of a *subjective truth* confirms that there is less a *separation* than an *interweaving* of theory and delusion. This formulation should not lead us to regard every theorist as a dangerous madman, or to judge any sort of raving as worthy of interest, but it should prompt us to think differently about the way that delusion and theory have certain affinities. We must keep in mind that the utopian belief in a clean separation between delusion and theory may lead to another kind of thought pathology: a lack of recognition—indeed, a radical denial—of the fundamental place of the subject.

Psychoanalytic theory, as Freud's examples suggest, seems to raise most clearly the question of the *entanglement* of delusion and theory. Not only does it place us in the shifting framework of the human sciences, but it has certain features that seem to predispose it to delusion. As such, psychoanalysis offers a particularly interesting position from which to reflect on the place of madness in thought.

First, this theory—of Freud and those who came after him—is quite original in the way it sustains a privileged bond with the person who conceived it. This bond is surely different from the one that attaches a physicist to the discoverer of a physical law, or scholars in the human sciences to the founders of their disciplines. So the question of objectivity is posed in a unique way, since it is inextricably mingled with that of filiation.

Moreover, it is not clear that we are dealing here with a theory that is comparable to any other.[7] Its concepts have their own status, since a complete understanding of them implies a personal effort of thought, indeed of analysis, on the part of the person who wishes to grasp their full meaning. For Freud, approaching psychoanalytic writing was almost inseparable from serious work on the self. All conceptual organization is defined here as the horizon of a subjective resistance that is at once its boundary and its object.

These "concepts" also display a flexibility that makes them adaptable to multiple contexts, as if extending them made them especially flexible and favorable to all sorts of interventions. Hence the frequently made—and not unfounded—reproach against psychoanalysis, that it can be applied to any situation or cultural production, as if the language of Freud were its natural expression.

Psychoanalytic theory's capacity for adaptability hardly serves to strengthen it, but rather gives it a fragility that can lead to madness. For psychoanalysis is most clearly linked to delusion by the fixed place it gives to the mechanism of interpretation. Searching for clues and making deductions, it tends, like delusion, to unveil another reality concealed behind the falseness of appearances. So it is permanently menaced by one of the psychic formations it is most suited (by vocation) to understand but to which it can never be completely external, since it is animated by an identical quest for meaning.

For all these reasons, psychoanalytic theory—and beyond that, the practices of reading related to it—grants a larger place to the subject than any other human science. And ever faithful to itself, it will be inclined to see evidence of unconscious activity at the heart of all thought, even shared thought. Whatever the insoluble contradictions to which such a recognition leads, this subjective portion is crucial to a Freudian perspective. It provides a model, even in its themes and its inner rhythms, to the questions we address to the world.

As in the previous chapter, we arrive at the conclusion that *delusion is subjective*, but we now give this formula a somewhat different meaning. Delusion is subjective not only because its identity depends on a particular person, but because it represents that part of ourselves which others cannot reach, and which, secretly concealed at the heart of our theoretical mythology, marks our individual effort to produce meaning.

CHAPTER 4

DELUSION AND CRITICISM

The question of delusion—whether in a theory as a whole or in a particular interpretation—is raised concretely in the case that concerns us here, which is the guilt of Dr. Sheppard. We are dealing with a novel, or written document, which everyone can agree with or not, as he likes. How are we to understand the question of delusion when we find ourselves faced not with a historical fact, public or private, or even with a metaphysical hypothesis, but with a literary text, and perhaps more broadly, with a work of art?

What status do we grant to the proposition that Dr. Sheppard may be innocent? This seems to be a false proposition—whatever the ultimate solution to our mystery—since it does not conform to the book's apparent conclusion. And it may even seem delusional if this judgment appears to be prompted by the intensity of our conviction.

As reviewed in the preceding chapter, the defining feature of delusion, even if it does not sum up its complexity or allow an unerring identification, is that it distorts reality. Now, the reality described by a literary text, while borrowing a great deal from the reality of the human world, can be distinguished from it on several points.[1]

One essential difference concerns the notion of *closure*. A literary text is reduced to a limited number of closed statements. This limitation separates literary reality from the realities of our world and, for example, from historical reality. While the knowledge of historical reality can be enriched by new documents, the reality of a literary work is strictly bound by its constituent statements. The possibilities of integrating preliminary notes and earlier drafts does not basically alter this fact, even if it allows us to confirm or dismiss certain hypotheses.

As soon as we accept this point, the nature of critical delusion comes into sharper focus. A delusional text is a text that goes beyond the statements that constitute the work and put a limit to critical madness. Moreover, it would be easy enough to invent statements of this type by asserting, for instance, that the Princesse de Clèves marries the Duc de Nemours, or that the narrator of Proust's *In Search of Lost Time* decides to devote himself to classical dance. Perhaps we would be wise to ascertain whether the other defining features of delusion are also present, especially the inner certainty of the person making such assertions. Yet even so we would be sure that these were completely false, if not delusional, statements (delusion implying a particular personal investment).

Unfortunately, things are not so simple. As an evident barrier to delusion, textual closure is a *material closure* that is not matched, however, by a *subjective closure*. What does this mean?

Let us observe, first of all, that it is easy enough to separate a true statement ("The Princesse de Clèves renounces the Duc de Nemours") from a false statement ("The Princesse de Clèves marries the Duc de Nemours") when we are dealing with readings of the text that repeat it in more or less literal paraphrase. Leaving aside interpretive criticism (how true are statements about the Princesse's unconscious masochism?), even the slightest psychological analysis quickly goes beyond the written statements and yields to suppositions that the text perhaps encourages but does not authorize, strictly speaking. In brief, sticking exclusively to what the text *says* may lead to solid but impoverished readings.

Another infraction of the idea of textual closure is the series of contradictions a text may involve. The most obvious cases figure in texts that are not reread, as when Proust recounts the death of Bergotte only to make him reappear several pages later. But other, more discreet contradictions often figure in narrative texts. This is our view of Agatha Christie's book, which produces a particular type of unresolvable contradiction—encouraged by the detective genre—by making the narrator an entirely separate character. The reader is then forced to choose among the different possibilities that the text offers him—in other words, not to believe all its statements. He is compelled to make choices.

But most important, *the world produced by the literary text is an incomplete world*, even if certain works propose worlds more complete than others. It would be more correct to speak of *fragments of worlds*, made up of parts of characters and dialogues, in which entire swaths of reality are missing. And—a crucial point—these blackouts in the world of the work are not due to a lack of information that may one day be supplied by research, as in the case of historical texts, but to a structural defect, namely that *this world does not suffer from a lost wholeness since it never was complete*. Due to this fact, the text is not legible if the reader does not give it its ultimate shape—for example, by consciously or unconsciously imagining a multitude of details that are not directly provided.

For all these reasons, there is no literary text independent of the subjectivity of the person who reads it. It is utopian to think that an objective text might exist onto which different readers would project themselves. And if this text did exist, it would be impossible, unfortunately, to grasp it without passing through the prism of subjectivity. It is the reader who completes the work and brings to a close the world it opens, and he does this each time in a different way.

The literary text's lack of independence in relation to the reader is particularly striking when it comes to characters.

Obviously, it would be desirable for a literary character to be limited, as Gerard Genette expressed the wish, "to the totality of statements by which the narrative signifies [him]."[2] While subscribing to such rigor is admirable, literary characters nonetheless seem to have a way of living an autonomous existence midway between the text and the subjectivity of the person who reads it.

Such an observation is not very original, and many critics would probably agree that every reader has "his" Sheppard, just as he has "his" Hamlet—divergences bringing to light the aspect of subjectivity that intervenes in the constitution of a character. Less banal, perhaps, is the claim that, from a psychoanalytic perspective, this aspect becomes the determining factor. It is true that this will be the case just as much for real persons, apart from the fact that the nonclosure of our world—which no written text limits—increases the possibilities of refining, indeed of modifying, our knowledge of beings.

This incompleteness of the world of the work invites the thought that a whole *intermediate world* exists around every character that is partly conscious and partly unconscious, produced by the limited nature of statements and the impossibility of increasing the available data. In relation to this world, the reader's calculations are developed so that the work, once completed, might achieve autonomy. Another world is created in a space governed by its own laws, more mobile and more personal than the text itself, but indispensable to its achievement of a minimal coherence in its unlimited series of encounters with the reader.

Granted, this has far-reaching consequences and prompts us to complete works indefinitely, attributing unknown lovers to the Princesse de Clèves or killing her with poison. But it is true that our creativity, at least our conscious creativity, is limited in its excess by one essential factor: our belief in the good faith of the narrator. If we refrain from imagining the vast intermediary world between the world of the work and our own, it is because we assume that a tacit pact exists whereby the narrator would conceal nothing crucial from us, or would not be a character like any other. Imagine how we would read literary texts written by an impersonal narrator if we set about systematically suspecting his good faith.[3]

The Murder of Roger Ackroyd is unique in the way the narrator's lie by omission conceals the most important fact of the story. Since the watertight barrier between the world of the text and the world that surrounds it has vanished, there is every reason to wonder whether other events are not also being concealed from us. From then on, the world of the work is no longer limited to its statements but extends well beyond them. This is all the more so, as we have seen, because this novel merely exemplifies, in caricature, a phenomenon involving the whole narrative of the detective thriller, namely, the narrator's bad faith.

Exceptionally visible in the case of Agatha Christie's book, this intermediary world remains present, indeed vital, around every literary work, even when we consciously refrain from exploring its terrain. The closure of the literary text is mere appearance. Far from underwriting this closure, limiting the number of statements only increases the reader's participation. Thus the text is constituted in a rather significant way by the individual reactions of all those who encounter it and animate it with their presence.

From the moment that we grant this essential difference between the real world and the imaginary world—whatever the numerous passages that link them together—it seems that each obeys a different type of truth and that the notion of delusion is not equally applicable.

In other words, by surrendering to the discourse that describes them, the real world and the imaginary world set in motion distinct types of undecidability. Imaginary worlds are not the exclusive preserve of uncertainty, as open as they may be to imagination. The real world, despite its predictability, also has its share of the unfathomable. But uncertainty is not deployed in each case according to the same logic.

For this reason, we would be inclined to suggest—taking up a distinction proposed by Tzvetan Todorov—that the world of the work is more familiar with the *truth of disclosure* than with the *truth of adequation*:

> We must distinguish between at least two senses of the word [truth]: truth-adequation and truth-disclosure; the former can be measured only against all or nothing, and the latter against more and less. It is either true or false that X has committed a crime, whatever the extenuating circumstances; the same can be said regarding whether or not Jews were incinerated at Auschwitz. If, however, the question involves the causes of Nazism or the identity of the average French person in 1991, no answer of this nature can be conceived: the answers can only contain more or less truth, since they endeavor to reveal the nature of a phenomenon, not to establish facts. Novelists aim only for this latter type of truth; nor do they have anything to teach the historian about the former.[4]

The advantage of this distinction is not to force overly strict dichotomies. The two truths can operate, to differing degrees, in both worlds, which in any case share certain similarities.[5] A significant number of elements of a text—notably historical texts—fall under adequation, and disclosure is at work in numerous statements about the real world. But this distinction happily allows us to avoid the binary choice between true and false when we are dealing with the imaginary world of a literary work.

Todorov's example is even more interesting in its application to crimes. A historical crime is a *fact* committed by a particular person independently of any written document or any contradiction in the documents. Even if the murderer eludes justice or the historical data, the crime has still taken place. A literary crime exists only in the statements that refer to it. If these are contradictory, there is no hope of bringing a truth to light that has nothing else to sustain it.

We see that the truth of disclosure dominates the field of literary criticism and so modifies our possible conception of a delusional reading, or, more simply, a false reading. An interpretive reading is justified, or conversely invalidated, less by a "reality" of the text—even if this clearly intervenes—than by the way this proposed reading is welcomed by its subsequent receivers[6] in a ceaseless movement of critical follow-up.

Now, Freud's tendency when he reads literary works is to *hammer the truth of disclosure onto the truth of adequation,*[7] so marked is the Freudian model by the image of the detective story. In this sense, his reading of *Oedipus Rex* establishes both a certain kind of literary criticism and a certain vision of psychoanalysis centered on trauma and mystery. Solid enough for Sophocles' play—which supports an Oedipal reading, even if Oedipus is innocent—Freud's reading is more questionable for other literary works, such as *Hamlet*, when it claims to subject the multiplicity of their virtual meanings to the constraining logic of a truth of adequation.

This *confusion of truths* allows us to grasp most clearly the detective model's hold on psychoanalysis and the way it runs the danger of making the rigors of adequation prevail in its image of the truth. Freud's reading of literary texts, whether detective stories or not, abundantly shows that he locates their referent in the real world, or in an imaginary world with identical laws, not in an incomplete world waiting to be read. In this sense, the search for the real killer of Laius or Roger Ackroyd is not limited to a parlor game but leads, outside the logic of adequation, to rethinking both literature and psychoanalysis by reminding ourselves of the specificity of the literary universe.

To privilege the truth of adequation in interpretive reading amounts to considering that the statements produced refer to something true or false, like real murders, whatever our success in finding the responsible parties. And such a privileging misjudges the way a literary work is modeled on the whim of each subjective universe—the only place where it comes to closure—by underestimating the place of the subject. Present in every inquiry, even a scientific one, the subject of this personal delusion allows us to construct meaning through the writing of our own private version.

That every theory may involve elements of delusion appears more clearly, then, in literary interpretation due to the insistent presence of that intermediary world in which the solitary reader completes the work and makes it his own. This world is populated by personal referents, sensitive to each person's story and unequal to anyone else's, and so establishes points of impenetrable incomprehension at the heart of all critical communication.

Thus the term delusion—with the personal implication we have given it—ends by losing its critical or polemical justification. To treat a reading as delusional because it lacks such textual truth, or would impose its own truth against all probability, would lead us to neglect the essential instability of the literary work and give free rein to the real pathologies of reading that challenge this instability. For this reason, in the field of literary interpretation, we are not dealing with authentic delusion but with necessarily subjective feelings about whether a proposed reading is admissible or not.

Far from discouraging us, these conclusions can only increase our determination to solve the mystery we've posed. For if it is true that an intermediary world exists between the text and the reader, it is likely that the murderer of Roger Ackroyd has found refuge there. He has been living there secretly, perhaps, since the creation of the work, in a deceptive tranquillity that is about to end.

PART IV

TRUTH

CHAPTER 1

CURTAIN

In 1946, scarcely midway in her career, Agatha Christie
drafted a secret manuscript which she deposited in her safe,
with instructions that it be published only after her death. This
novel recounts Hercule Poirot's final investigation.[1] He is
therefore in the same anachronistic position as in *The Murder
of Roger Ackroyd*, in which Dr. Sheppard mentions the detective's retirement. But this time the story is told by his loyal
companion, the irreproachable Hastings.

Curtain unfolds in Styles once again, where Poirot and Hastings conducted their first investigation,[2] in the very house
where the earlier crime took place and which has now become
a boarding house. Poirot, gravely ill and close to death, sum-
mons Hastings, whose daughter is also present, to come and
help him solve his last case. He explains to Hastings that this
time the two detectives are faced with a dangerous murderer
who commits his murders so deftly that it is impossible to stop
him.

This is the first peculiarity of *Curtain*: the originality of the
murders. The criminal, a certain Norton, understands what all
of Agatha Christie's novels tend to demonstrate: that *we are all
potential murderers* who restrain our impulse to kill. This is
what Poirot explains to Hastings in the last letter he sends him,
a letter in which he explains Norton's method:

> Now you must realize this, Hastings. *Everyone is a po-
> tential murderer*—in everyone there arises from time to
> time the *wish* to kill—though not the *will* to kill. How

often have you not felt or heard others say: "She made me so furious I could have killed her!" — "I could have killed B. for saying so-and-so!". . . And all those statements are literally true. Your mind at such moments is quite clear. You would like to kill so-and-so. *But you do not do it.* Your will has to assent to your desire.[3]

Norton's technique consists precisely of inciting the will. Inspired by the method practiced by Iago in *Othello*, Norton does not kill directly, but *through his influence.* Locating a more or less conscious desire in certain people to kill someone close to them, he goes about helping to foster that desire—out of pure sadism. Poirot continues:

So then, we are all potential murderers. And the art of X [Norton] was this: not to suggest the *desire*, but to break down the normal decent resistance. It was an art perfected by long practice. [Norton] knew the exact word, the exact phrase, the intonation even to suggest and to bring cumulative pressure on a weak spot! It could be done. It was done without the victim ever suspecting. It was not hypnotism—hypnotism would not have been successful. It was something more insidious, more deadly. It was a marshalling of the forces of a human being to widen a breach instead of repairing it (Postscript, 255).

Living in the Styles boarding house, the murderer begins his work of destruction, and the results are not long in coming. Hastings is seized by the wish to poison a seducer with whom his daughter seems to have fallen in love. Another resident of the boarding house, Colonel Luttrell, comes close to killing his wife—who took pleasure in publicly humiliating him—with a rifle. Finally, a third resident of the boarding house, Mrs. Franklin, is poisoned.

Sensing that the killer is on the verge of committing other murders, Poirot decides to intervene. He invites Norton to his apartment, reveals to him that he knows about his activities, and puts him to sleep with a cup of hot chocolate containing a sedative. Then he takes him back to his room and shoots him in the head.[4]

So Hercule Poirot's final investigation is dedicated to telling how he himself has become a murderer:

> Yes, my friend, it is odd—and laughable—and terrible! I, who do not approve of murder—I, who value human life—have ended my career by committing murder. Perhaps it is because I have been too self-righteous, too conscious of rectitude—that this terrible dilemma has come to me. For you see, Hastings, there are two sides to it. It is my work in life to save the innocent—to *prevent* murder—and this—this is the only way I can do it! Make no mistake—[Norton] could not be touched by the law. He was safe. By no ingenuity that I could think of could he be defeated any other way. (Postscript, 256).[5]

If justifications for this execution are not lacking, it must be observed that the revelation of Poirot's guilt exemplifies the axiom on which Norton's murderous activity rests: Each of us is a potential murderer. Poirot himself does not seem to contradict this when, at the end of his letter, he displays less confidence in the legitimacy of his act: "Eh bien, I have no more now to say. I do not know, Hastings, if what I have done is justified or not justified. No—I do not know. . . . But now I am very humble and I say like a little child: 'I do not know'" (Postscript, 278-79).

So the book rests on the classic narrative ploy of every detective novel: The most unlikely suspect is the killer. As the mythic figure of the investigator, Poirot is the most unlikely suspect among all the characters, since he is proscribed from killing by his function. In this respect, the book resembles *The*

Murder of Roger Ackroyd, the only difference being that this time it is the other investigator, Poirot himself, who is presented as guilty.

We should examine even more carefully what Norton and Poirot are asserting when they both demonstrate (Poirot by killing, Norton by inciting others to kill) that each of us is a potential murderer. The figure of the detective killer is not limited to rehearsing a classic method of disguise, but insists, by dramatic illustration, on every person's potential guilt. In the absence of any exception to the rule of generalized suspicion, this figure lays blame, as a result, on the very principle of narration.

The fact that Poirot himself—the supreme referent of the detective narrative—can commit a murder makes the text once again inconclusive (what faith can we grant the testimony of a man who boasts of murdering someone who has not committed a crime?). More important, it makes any narrative impossible, since a narrative implies, as a guarantee of its authenticity, a position external to the crime where the law, which is also the law of organizing facts, might be spoken.

This impossibility of the narrative is confirmed by the second surprise in Poirot's posthumous letter. Rarely short of ideas, the detective informs Hastings, after confessing his own murder, that—surprise—Hastings too is a murderer.

Going back to the death of Mrs. Franklin, Poirot reveals in his posthumous letter to his loyal confidant that Hastings killed her without realizing it:

> And now we come to the death of Barbara Franklin. Whatever your ideas may be on the subject, Hastings, I do think you have once suspected the truth.
>
> For you see, Hastings, it was *you* killed Barbara. *Mais oui*, you did! (Postscript, 268)

The victim, Mrs. Franklin, married to a physician who prefers scientific research to social events, is in love with the diplomat Boyd Carrington, who loves her in return. Falling under Norton's pernicious influence, she decides to get rid of her husband by poisoning him with the product he uses for his work and making it look as though he swallowed it inadvertently.

The evening of the murder, Hastings is with Mrs. Franklin in her room, in the presence of her husband and several other residents of the boarding house who have gathered for coffee. Mrs. Franklin, who is ill, is lying in bed. Her cup is near her, on top of a small revolving bookcase, and her husband's cup—with the poison—is next to him on the other side.

Suddenly, shooting stars are seen in the sky. Everyone rushes to the window to watch them, except for Hastings, who is lost in his thoughts and turns the bookcase looking for a citation from Shakespeare's *Othello*, a volume located on the other side. Poirot goes on:

And so they come back and Mrs. Franklin drinks the coffee full of the Calabar bean alkaloids that were meant for dear scientific John, and John Franklin drinks the nice plain cup of coffee that was meant for clever Mrs. Franklin.

But you will see, Hastings, if you think a minute, that although I realized what had happened . . . I could not *prove* what had happened (Postscript, 271).

So in the same book in which Poirot confesses to a crime, Hastings discovers that he, too, has committed one, and the detective duo are revealed, in their final investigation, to be a pair of murderers.

Now, if we pay close attention, this discovery takes place at the reading of Poirot's posthumous letter, a document that figures at the end of the novel and couldn't have been previously known to the narrator. As a result, the narrative of the murder, coming long before the reading of Poirot's letter, is a fake narrative in which the involuntary killer recounts how he became guilty of murder without telling the reader. He does not say so for the simple reason that he is unaware of it. As in *The Murder of Roger Ackroyd* and *Endless Night*, the reader is therefore invited to be an unwitting witness to the description of a murder by its author, with the difference that *the narrator himself does not know, as he tells his story, that he has committed it.*

The narrative organization of the book makes it difficult to say whether Hastings is lying by omission or not, since the category has become inadequate. On the one hand, there was clearly an omission, with the narrator, like Sheppard or Michael Rogers, avoiding any mention of the murder. But on the other hand, there is no real omission because Hastings does not know that he has committed murder: Omission implies preexisting knowledge. Hence we have the unlikely narrative situation in which Hastings finds himself led to recount in detail an act that he is unaware of having committed.

It is not so much the classic method of the lie by omission that is used here—in this book defying every theory of narrative—as a very subtle way of disseminating information that makes it not illegible but meaningless. While the evening of the murder seems devoted to trivial conversations, everything is actually played out around the positions of the people and coffee cups in the room. And even these basic elements, taken separately, are incomprehensible.

So we are told of Dr. Franklin that, "seated on the other side of the revolving bookcase," he was ". . . handing the cups [to his wife] as she filled them" (XIII, 181). Lost in the description of the evening, this sentence seems perfectly anecdotal. Should we decide to pay attention, the crucial fact would not appear, namely that Dr. Franklin and his wife are sitting on opposite sides of the revolving bookcase.

A little further on, the criminal gesture is completely invisible, although it is described in detail. While the other occupants of the room, having noticed the shooting stars, rush over to the balcony and Dr. Franklin carries his wife in his arms through the French doors, Hastings stays in the room, melancholy at the thought of his own dead wife:

> I remained with my head bent over the crossword . . . for I was remembering . . . a clear tropical night . . . a shooting star. I was standing there by the window, and I had turned and picked up Cinders [his young wife] and carried her out in my arms to see the stars and wish . . .
>
> The lines of the crossword ran and blurred before my eyes (XIII, 182–83).

At this moment, Hastings' daughter appears:

> A figure detached itself from the balcony and came into the room—Judith.
>
> Judith must never catch me with tears in my eyes. Hastily I swung round the bookcase and pretended to be looking for a book. I remembered having seen an old edition of Shakespeare there. Yes, here it was. I looked through *Othello*.

We might think that the murder is described in the phrase, "I swung round the bookcase." But the method is still more complex. For it is not by turning the bookcase *but by not putting it back as it was* that Hastings does the killing. The murder is designated by that absent phrase, which no reader could possibly notice, first of all because it is absent and then because at this stage of the reading, he has no reason to take any interest in the position of bookcases.

As with every poisoning, the accomplishment of the murder takes a certain amount of time:

The others were coming back, laughing and talking. Mrs. Franklin resumed her place on the chaise longue. Franklin came back to his seat and stirred his coffee. Norton and Elizabeth Cole finished drinking theirs and excused themselves, as they had promised to play bridge with the Luttrells.

Mrs. Franklin drank her coffee and then demanded her "drops." Judith got them for her from the bathroom (XIII, 184).

This time, the murder is consummated and Hastings, at the very moment when Mrs. Franklin drinks her coffee—and only at that moment, since he never thought to commit murder—*has become* a murderer.

Because of its status as a posthumous text and through the double revelation that the two detectives have been transformed into criminals, Poirot's last investigation casts an odd light on the other works. The separation between good and evil tends to blur. On the one hand, the killer Norton does not commit a crime, strictly speaking, or commits crimes that are not recognized as such by the law. In contrast, the two detectives, Poirot more than Hastings, have both become murderers.

Compared to the preceding works, which pit truth against lie, this third, dark version of *The Murder of Roger Ackroyd* constructs a murky universe with vague moral boundaries. The fantasy that underlies all the works, that the detective himself might commit murder, is realized this time, and doubly so, with the characters who are supposed to respect law and order giving in to unlawful acts for excellent reasons.

But beyond this first transgression, a second comes to light that involves the narrative act of stating and completely destabilizes it. First, Poirot appears here as an ambivalent figure, his guilt prohibiting him, in this investigation—as it does retroactively in the others—from occupying the moral or narrative high ground.[6] More crucial still, because *the hypothesis of unconscious acts prevents any access to a truth about the self*, Hastings is a narrator who lies. But, unlike Dr. Sheppard, he is unaware that he is lying, thereby leaving the reading utterly open-ended.

Opening literary works to the world outside, the lie by omission—coupled with the hypothesis of the characters' unconscious—takes on a new significance and an unlimited reach. It no longer corresponds, as with Ackroyd or Michael Rogers, to what the characters refuse to acknowledge, since they lie without any prior knowledge. Having lost any specific meaning, this lie comes to stand for everything the characters do not know about themselves, an Other Scene (one of Freud's terms for the unconscious) that effectively invalidates any equivalence between speech and reality. By this radical corruption of the act of reference, any possibility of completing the text is invalidated, too.

With Hastings' crime—committed by a man who is honesty itself—the construct of the detective story is radically ruptured. We are reminded that every narrator is a character, the source of a point of view on the world, not of a transcendent truth: How could the invisible narrator who organizes certain fictions be more reliable than Hastings? In the world of the detective novel, in which everyone lies, there is no absolute knowledge but only the remnants of partial truths. It is not insignificant that Hastings' lies are revealed in the same book as the murder by Poirot, since these are the two faces of an identical transgression. The major violation of the law (he who is entrusted with upholding it, flouts it) is matched by another transgression that concerns language: No literary site exists where the truth can be spoken, because every truth is produced by a subject.

More than *Endless Night*, perhaps, *Curtain* demonstrates, with the figure of a criminal who does not actually commit the crime, how the detective novel is not the site of a truth of adequation but the site of a truth of disclosure, making any closure utopian. Far from providing this hermeneutic model with an inscribed meaning of the sort that psychoanalysis makes use of, the detective novel opens itself up to multiple readings called forth by the contradictions provoked by the multiplicity of words and the definitive absence of any omniscient narrator. In this way, it appeals to the creative act of reading.

CHAPTER 2

THE TRUTH

One condition must now be stated before proposing our hypothesis on the death of Roger Ackroyd. Original solutions are not lacking, and the one Poirot proposes quite seriously—that the murderer would have paid a visit to his victim carrying a receptacle containing a dagger, a pair of shoes, and a dictaphone transformed into an alarm clock, before going home to wait for the steward's telephone call, then returning to the scene of the crime to move a high-backed chair—stimulates our own creativity. We might rival the detective and imagine, in a similar style, solutions according to which Ackroyd committed suicide by contorting himself to stab the dagger into the back of his own neck, or by inventing an ingenious device that would throw the weapon at him from a distance. The image of the killer's receptacle, which seems unusually capacious, would also allow for interesting variations. As for the dictaphone, it would be tempting to perfect it by giving it a remote control.

However, we will confine ourselves to serious hypotheses that fall within the logic of the book and of the body of work to which it refers, a logic that seems contradicted by the accepted solution identifying Dr. Sheppard as the killer. We proscribe any delusional or poetic solution, so as to stay within the arid limits of rigor and respond simply to our initial question: Who killed Roger Ackroyd?

We have identified two likely killers. The first is the person the book denounces and who has been passed on to posterity as such: Dr. Sheppard. The second is the person who looks most guilty before Poirot produces his solution: Ralph Paton.

Each of these solutions has its pros and cons. We are familiar with the novelistic advantage of Dr. Sheppard as killer: His
identification creates the effect of surprise in numerous readers. But the drawbacks are not trivial: He hardly has a criminal's psychology, his motives are dubious, it is rather unlikely
that he could have physically committed the murder, and his
attitude during and after the investigation is strange.

With Ralph Paton, the situation is reversed. He has the
necessary psychological profile, his motive is solid, and he was
remarkably well positioned to kill Ackroyd, as he readily acknowledges. But a solution that would lead to accusing him is
disappointing from a narrative viewpoint, since from the beginning of the book Paton seemed the most likely killer.

Hence the temptation to seek out a character who would
combine the advantages of both Sheppard and Paton without
their disadvantages. Who would (or could) surprise the reader
as much as Sheppard, have a more solid motive, a psychology
more in line with the act, and, above all, the physical possibility of committing the murder?

We are going to review the different elements of the investigation, demonstrating, as Poirot does, that all the facts lead
irresistibly toward the same conclusion. And so we will be in a
position to say, like him: "I will take you the way I have
traveled myself. Step by step you shall accompany me, and see
for yourself that all the facts point indisputably to one person"
(XXV, 243).

The search for the murderer can be made in two general di-
rections represented by the two suspects mentioned. Either the
murder is linked to the death of Mrs. Ferrars, or it has nothing
to do with it. Sheppard is emblematic of the first solution,
Ralph Paton of the second, since he cannot be accused of
blackmailing Mrs. Ferrars.

There is one compelling reason why we, like Poirot, judge
that Ackroyd's murder is indeed linked to the death of Mrs.

Ferrars: the disappearance from Ackroyd's study of the letter, whose existence is confirmed by two witnesses, Sheppard and Parker. Like Poirot, even if we think that he is mistaken in his reasoning, we shall infer that the goal of the murder was the disappearance of the letter and the person who had read it.

A first feature of our murderer begins to emerge: It is someone close to Ferrars—in other words, someone from the village. This immediately eliminates potential suspects like Charles Kent (the son of Elizabeth Russell) or Major Blunt. Since neither of them lives in the region, it seems difficult to imagine that they would have known the circumstances of Mrs. Ferrars' death and had the physical means to blackmail her over a long period of time. This also exonerates Hercule Poirot (who, as we have just seen, is capable of murder), who has just settled in the village.

Another direction of inquiry concerns the personality of the murderer. Obviously, we are dealing with someone very determined, the complete opposite of the insipid Dr. Sheppard. The speed—less than a day—with which the murder was planned and executed suggests someone deliberate, implacable, and sure of himself. Naturally, this portrait is valid only if we follow the hypothesis that the murder is linked to the blackmail of Mrs. Ferrars, but this is the hypothesis we have chosen to adopt.

These psychological elements are not adequate to identify the murderer, but they allow us to eliminate characters from the list of suspects who do not fit this description, such as Flora Ackroyd, her mother Mrs. Cecil Ackroyd, or Geoffrey Raymond, Ackroyd's secretary. On the other hand, we are left with a number of characters who do fit, such as Parker, who is already a proven blackmailer. As for Major Blunt, the big-game hunter and adventurer, he would correspond nicely to this profile, but since he was already eliminated above, he no longer figures among our suspects.

*   *   *

The third direction of inquiry concerns the performance of the murder itself. First, the killer must have been in a position to take the weapon from Ackroyd's silver table. In fact, the circumstances of its disappearance remain vague, and our chief testimony, namely Sheppard's, is subject to caution.[1] The theft of the dagger therefore does not seem to be a decisive factor in trapping the murderer.

Did the murderer come from inside or outside the house? This question is crucial. Remember, we have adopted a hypothesis in which Sheppard is not the killer. So a basic piece of information to which Poirot—for good reason—attaches little importance becomes central: On the evening of the murder, Ackroyd does not want to be disturbed (IV, 48). He gives instructions to this effect to Parker, indirectly through Sheppard, and Ackroyd is no doubt the person who locks his study door.

Several supplementary pieces of information then emerge. First of all, *the person whom Ackroyd receives that evening, and who leaves his footprints behind, comes from outside the house*: It cannot be someone from inside the house, since Ackroyd would be unlikely to open the window trustingly to someone living under his own roof. Our portrait is therefore enriched by an additional decisive feature, which this time eliminates in one fell swoop almost all the characters in the book gathered this evening in Ackroyd's house: The murderer does not live in Ackroyd's house and is not present at dinner. It is possible, but not certain, that Ackroyd has agreed to meet him. In any case, it is someone whom he has every reason to trust or whom he considers harmless.

What time was the murder committed? If Sheppard is innocent, Ackroyd was still alive at around nine o'clock. *In any case, the murder takes place much later*, since—the hypothesis of the dictaphone vanishes with the guilt of Dr. Sheppard—it is really Ackroyd's voice that the witnesses hear. In fact, the exact time of the crime ceases in our view to be a decisive element in identifying the murderer, who, in any case, has plenty of time to act.

A fourth avenue of inquiry concerns the question of information. If we follow the hypothesis of a link between the blackmail of the victimized Mrs. Ferrars and the murder, then information—as in every case of blackmail—is the major key.

This comes into play on several levels. First, the blackmailer, whether he is the murderer or not, knows that Mrs. Ferrars has poisoned her husband. On this point, as Poirot notes, Sheppard is the best placed: "Who could have had a better knowledge of what killed Mr. Ferrars than the doctor who was attending him?" (XXVI, 250) Even so, Sheppard is not the only villager to procure such information.

Information comes into play on a second point. How could the murderer know that Mrs. Ferrars had sent a letter to Ackroyd? This is a crucial question, for the killer—who certainly planned his crime—could only do so by knowing that a threat was to come from Mrs. Ferrars. Sheppard was not aware of this, even if he says he suspected it.

On the other hand, what Sheppard could not know—and here lies the major fault in Poirot's argument—is that Mrs. Ferrars sent *only one letter* (and did not warn the police, for example) and that killing Ackroyd therefore makes sense. We can be sure that the person who possesses this crucial information is the murderer.

A fifth direction of inquiry concerns the reader and the revelation of the truth. As in every detective story of this type, the discovery of the murderer must be a surprise. Our task, then, is to find someone whom no one suspects, even when—and we refer here again to the Van Dine principle—this murderer is always in plain view.

Few characters in the book conform to this description. According to this criterion, and for reasons stated above, it is clear that after Sheppard, Hercule Poirot himself is next on the list. This hypothesis is not impossible, but it is quite implausible since, unlike the scenario in *Curtain*, he has no motive (clearly, as we have seen, he cannot be the blackmailer). As for the other investigators, such as Inspector Raglan, they are too dull to rise to the level of the Machiavellian killer who has conceived and executed Ackroyd's murder. We can, however, assume that without really being an investigator, the murderer is closely involved in the investigation.

Now for a recapitulation: It is clear that the murderer is someone who is part of the story although no one suspects him; someone with great inner strength who, not being present at Ackroyd's dinner party, could go looking for the dagger in the silver table, then knock on Ackroyd's French door for him to open up; someone remarkably well informed about village life, capable, for example—thanks to a private network of connections—of knowing everything about the death of Ferrars and his wife, and of observing their postman. In a name: Caroline Sheppard.

CHAPTER 3

NOTHING BUT THE TRUTH

One immediate objection comes to mind. In our hypothesis, even if Caroline Sheppard were in a position to commit the murder, she has no apparent motive. Unless we assume, which is rather unlikely for anyone who knows her psychology and her way of life, that she herself was blackmailing Mrs. Ferrars.

To understand what has happened, we must add two details that perceptibly modify our point of view. First, there is no indication—if we assume a plot twist—that the murderer and the blackmailer are one and the same person. That Dr. Sheppard may have blackmailed Mrs. Ferrars does not prove that he is the murderer. This hypothesis, moreover, is evoked several times during the investigation, even by Poirot himself, who declares that he is prepared to disconnect the two transgressions but finally attributes them both to the same criminal (XV, 160; XVIII, 190).

Second, all indications suggest that this murder is what we call an *altruistic murder*: a murder that is not committed for the direct benefit of the killer, but for the benefit of someone whom the killer is protecting. In short, in the hypothesis we are now going to elaborate, Caroline Sheppard killed to protect her brother, who was the blackmailer.

To understand exactly what happened, we have to look at the whole text—something Hercule Poirot does not do, focusing as he does on a few secondary, even anecdotal elements—and what it is telling us when we are repeatedly informed that *Caroline Sheppard knows everything that happens in the village.*

If this is true, she is certainly informed of the circumstances of Ferrars' death and of her brother's blackmail operation. How could it be otherwise? How could this woman, who during the investigation had all the details at hand and kept track of everyone's movements, possibly be unaware that her brother was seeing Mrs. Ferrars regularly and blackmailing her for at least a year? And how could she fail to be surprised by the considerable sums of money that her brother, according to Poirot, has lost in speculations (XXVI, 250)? Similarly, it is unlikely that Sheppard could work out the practical details of Ackroyd's death without his sister, who spends her days spying on him, noticing what he is up to.

Caroline learns of Mrs. Ferrars' death before anyone else. Most important, she alone knows that Mrs. Ferrars had sent a letter—*and only one letter*—before her death (the book even provides the identity of her informant: the milkman who visits Mrs. Ferrars' cook [I, 13]). We have insisted on this major point: Only the person who has access to this information, which Sheppard would never have in his possession, has real reasons for killing.

What Caroline Sheppard may also guess is that her brother would never have the courage to commit a murder, even if the idea has crossed his mind. So she follows him that evening, or, more probably, she goes walking in the vicinity of Fernly Park. Concealing herself, she witnesses the conversation between her brother and Ackroyd from outside the house. It is her presence to which the text alludes when Ackroyd says that he feels watched, spied upon (IV, 47), a phrase that remains strangely forgotten in the final explanation: No one feels spied upon by someone standing beside him.

Perhaps Sheppard really did *intend* to kill Ackroyd, as he says in the last chapter of his manuscript ("I suppose I must have meant to murder him all along. As soon as I heard of Mrs. Ferrars' death . . ." [XXVII, 253]), and was even carrying a weapon ("I'd brought a handy little weapon of my own, but when I saw the dagger lying in the silver table, it occurred to me at once how much better it would be to use a weapon that couldn't be traced to me" [XXVII, 253]). But he certainly did not have the courage to use it—both for psychological reasons and because he could not be certain that this murder would serve its purpose—and Caroline, hidden near Ackroyd's study, helplessly witnesses his failure.

So she knocks at the French door. Ackroyd has no reason not to open it up for her, as she is coming from outside the house, and no reason to mistrust her, as it is not her name but her brother's that figures in the letter of denunciation. Quite the contrary, reeling from the shock of his new discovery, he has every reason to welcome her and no thought that she is coming to kill him, now that he knows the guilty party.

Caroline is therefore the mysterious visitor whom some residents of the house heard speaking with Ackroyd, and the woman glimpsed in the park by Major Blunt (IX, 102; XXIII, 234). This hypothesis is altogether simpler and more satisfying than that of a dictapone rigged to play automatically. Even more because the tenor of the statements overheard by the witnesses—the refusal to grant a request (to hush up the blackmail business)—entirely squares with the conversation we can imagine taking place between Ackroyd and Caroline.

What happens next? It is difficult to choose between two different hypotheses that allow both facts to coexist: Dr. Sheppard leaves Ackroyd alive and goes home around nine o'clock. One hour later, he has the feeling, even the conviction, that Ackroyd is dead and decides to return to the scene of the crime.

The telephone call is clearly not how Sheppard learns of Ackroyd's death. The investigation, whose conclusions must be respected in such cases, has shown that it was made by the steward. But the expected telephone call allows Sheppard to find a pretext for going back to Ackroyd's house, where he thinks that a murder has been committed, a murder for which he is not responsible. He wants to verify it or to eliminate its traces. Above all, the phone call allows him to observe Caroline's reactions and confirm whether there are any grounds for his fears. How does he know? We can think of several hypotheses, some of which are compatible. The simplest is that Sheppard, upon leaving Ackroyd's house, catches a glimpse of Caroline in the park or ponders the identity of the mysterious feminine shadow (also glimpsed by Major Blunt), and then stops or tries to approach her—which would explain the slight difference in chronology raised by Poirot.

Another solution: If Caroline truly committed the murder, she would not be at home when Sheppard returns, and he would be rightly surprised by this. The text certainly does not proscribe such a reading: "Ten minutes later I was at home once more. Caroline was full of curiosity to know why I had returned so early. I had to make up a slightly fictitious account of the evening in order to satisfy her, and I had an uneasy feeling that she saw through the transparent device" (IV, 49). Granting the prevalence throughout the narrative of the lie by omission, why not assume that the ellipses to which Sheppard refers might be situated between "I was at home once more" and "Caroline was full of curiosity"? Her surprise at seeing her brother come home so early is more understandable if she herself was out.

If Sheppard's attention was quite reasonably drawn to the fact that Caroline was late, another element could have suggested to him that Ackroyd was dead. As in the hypothesis in which Paton is the murderer, this is a matter not of a fact but of *the absence of a fact*, namely that Ackroyd does not telephone. How do we explain this if Sheppard, who is his best friend, is innocent? How can we fail to connect Ackroyd's strange telephonic silence with Caroline's lateness?

Finally, a last hypothesis: Sheppard knows that Ackroyd is dead because his sister tells him, admitting that she has committed the murder and explaining why she judged it necessary to get rid of Ackroyd. However, this hypothesis is less likely than the other three, for nothing in the numerous conversations between brother and sister suggests the existence of a shared secret.

In order to understand why Sheppard then rushes off to Ackroyd's, we must imagine that he is motivated by the same reasons as Caroline. This is the secret at the heart of the work: Sheppard and his sister are entirely devoted to one another and will do anything to protect each other. Without this hypothesis, numerous oddities of the text remain unexplained. Mutual protection leads them a great distance, to what can be called a double altruistic murder: Caroline kills to protect her brother, and he kills himself to save his sister.

As we might expect, this proposal contradicts Poirot's solution since it is constructed against it. The most important thing is whether or not it contradicts Sheppard's manuscript.

Let us remember, first of all, that Sheppard never confesses to the murder. On the contrary, the different formulas that allude to it seem deliberately chosen for their ambiguity. Mention is made of the intention to kill Ackroyd, or the respective merits of different weapons, but never the murder itself. Most of these statements can be read as having a double meaning, following the same principle that leads to the accusation of Sheppard as the killer, only in reverse. The sentence: "I'm always glad that I gave him a chance. I urged him to read that letter before it was too late" (XXVII, 253) is just as significant if Caroline is the murderer. That is even truer for this line, which insists on Sheppard's innocence: "He knew danger was close at hand. And yet he never suspected *me*."

In fact, the only statements that radically contradict our solution have to do with the dictaphone. After his meeting with Ackroyd, Sheppard says he went home after taking "precautions" (XXVII, 254). He then explains that Ackroyd, knowing his mechanical skill, had given him the device to repair: "I did what I wanted to it, and took it up with me in my bag that evening." These preparations announce the narrative of the murder, in which Sheppard returns to the dictaphone: "When I looked around the room from the door, I was quite satisfied. Nothing had been left undone. The dictaphone was on the table by the window, timed to go off at nine-thirty (the mechanism of that little device was rather clever—based on the principle of an alarm clock), and the arm-chair was pulled out so as to hide it from the door."

Finally, the dictaphone appears a third time in the narrative of the the crime's discovery: " '*I did what little had to be done!*' It was quite little—just to shove the dictaphone into my bag and push back the chair against the wall in its proper place" (XXVII, 255).

Without any proof of bad faith, it is undeniable that we come very close here to a confession. But these statements, as overwhelming as they seem at first glance, cannot be examined independently of the whole set of structural problems that the book poses, the chief one being our inclination to discredit the statements of a confessed liar. Above all, these statements concern the improbable hypothesis of the dictaphone—the most ridiculous part of Poirot's solution. If we regard Sheppard as innocent, it is tempting to see in his remarks an ironic missile aimed at the detective's intention.

If this reading has some drawbacks, it also offers certain advantages. One is that it is much simpler than the reading proposed by the novel. No need here to deal with a dictaphone, to move an armchair, or to steal a pair of shoes from an inn in the presence of their owner.[1]

It also offers a more coherent detective story. It avoids saddling someone with the crime who has no interest in committing it, who is physically unable to do it, who does not have the psychological capability, and who does everything possible to implicate himself.

This reading has—it is hoped—a certain beauty, since it transforms a sordid story of money into a story of love. For the whole murderous mechanism leading to the double demise of Ackroyd and Sheppard rests entirely on the passionate love between a brother and sister, each ready to do anything, even to kill, to save the other.

CHAPTER 4

THE WHOLE TRUTH

The solution to which this investigation of the book has led us, surprising as it may seem, is not completely unreasonable. It can be reached another way, this time by means of a more psychoanalytic reading. Attentive to other facts and another logic, such a reading is in the position to deliver a truth of the work that does not conform to the official truth, and that is closer to—and even largely confirms—what our own investigation has established.

Curiously, the truth of the work, far from being concealed, is located quite clearly in different strategic places. This is true from the very first page, in Sheppard's introduction of his sister: "The motto of the mongoose family, so Mr. Kipling tells us, is: 'Go and find out.' If Caroline ever adopts a crest, I should certainly suggest a mongoose rampant. One might omit the first part of the motto. Caroline can do any amount of finding out by sitting placidly at home" (I,11).

This comparison of Caroline to a mongoose does not seem trivial, since it is repeated several chapters further on. Caroline, walking through the woods ostensibly to admire the fall colors, overhears a conversation between Ralph Paton and Ursula Bourne, and her account of it draws these ironic remarks from her brother: "Caroline does not care a hang for woods at any time of year. Normally she regards them as places where you get your feet damp, and where all kinds of unpleasant things may drop on your head. No, it was good sound mongoose instinct which took her to our local wood. It is the only place adjacent to the village of King's Abbot where you can talk with a young woman unseen by the whole of the village" (III, 32).

In both cases, the analogy is motivated by Caroline's curiosity. But oddly, curiosity is not a crucial element in the Kipling text referred to, in all probability "Rikki-tikki-tavi," a story from *The Jungle Book*. Although curiosity is referred to at the beginning of that story ("The motto of all the mongoose family is 'Run and find out,' and Rikki-tikki was a true mongoose"),[1] the focus subsequently shifts away from it entirely in favor of two qualities that together sustain the plot.

Kipling's mongoose is first and foremost an animal who protects her home turf. Taken into the family by a little boy, Teddy, the animal sets about protecting the house from external attacks, and especially from snakes. She is able to do this because of a second quality: her remarkable *capacity to kill*. In several pages, Rikki-tikki exterminates no less than three adult snakes—including two cobras—and twenty-five small snakes.

The mongoose's murderous power is, moreover, not a peculiarity of Kipling's heroine. Besides corresponding to accepted scientific observation, it is mentioned as a characteristic feature in all the dictionaries and encyclopedias of the time—which make no reference to curiosity—so much so that it might pass as the defining feature of this animal.[2]

Is it conceivable that Sheppard, by this reference to an animal celebrated for its capacity to kill, has voluntarily dropped the name of the murderer? Or are we to think that this reference is unconscious? Is it, in any case, an even clearer formulation that appears on the final page of his confession: "My greatest fear all through has been Caroline" (XXVII, 255)?[3]

Such a strong formulation is difficult to understand if Sheppard is simply worried about Caroline's perspicacity. Everything happens as if the book were framed by a scarcely veiled double accusation, and as if the narrator could not refrain from discreetly fingering the real criminal in this text in which he falsely accuses himself.

*   *   *

How do we explain the fact that Caroline Sheppard is never a suspect, despite these nearly explicit accusations? She seems to occupy a singular place in the work, as if she were not subject to the same rules as the other characters and had the benefit, in relation to them, of exorbitant privileges.

Let us observe, first of all, a strange fact that illustrates to what extent her place is an uncommon one. At no time do the investigators—Hercule Poirot as well as the official police—suspect her *or even ask her to account for her whereabouts on the evening of the murder*. And the investigators' lack of curiosity is merely an extension of the narrator's, who never gives us the slightest indication of what Caroline was doing on the decisive evening.

Now, this point is quite singular and probably unique in all of Agatha Christie's work, where it is customary that every character's use of time, especially the least suspect, is verified in minute detail.[4] And it is all the more singular since Poirot's various reasonings, which lead him to what he thinks is the truth, are based on infinitesimal chronological discrepancies, such as the so-called unexplained five minutes in Sheppard's schedule.

Preemptorily excluded from the list of suspects, kept outside the frame of the story, Caroline Sheppard can then circulate freely in the village on the evening of the murder without having to account for herself to anyone, while all the other characters must justify their comings and goings down to the minute. Such freedom makes any question about her physical possibility of committing the murder useless: Unlimited by the constraints that weigh on the other suspects, she appears to be the very image of the all-powerful criminal.

This improbable freedom is poorly explained, unless we assume that the character is not really taken seriously by the text and is not considered an entirely separate actor. This is our impression of the figure of Caroline upon reading the book: a being at once very present on the phantasmic level and utterly disconnected from the specific details that traditionally anchor the most concrete protagonists of a detective novel to reality.

Attentive to such textual discrepancies, psychoanalysis also allows us to read the creatures of fiction not exclusively as characters but to consider entities that transcend them or surpass them: the psychic forces at play in the work. The mechanisms of displacement and condensation can summon phantasmic couples from established characters—composite figures that are otherwise unimaginable. This psychic geometry allows us a sharper glimpse of the relations among the three points of the triangle formed by Poirot, Sheppard, and his sister.

Resorting to this way of reading inspired by the dream, a first dyad can be seen that involves Sheppard and Caroline—a mirror-image couple, not so much based on sibling mimicry as on the parent/child relationship. For Caroline is the strong element in this couple that reminds us of mother and son. Occupied with keeping the doctor's house, preparing his meals, continually advising him, even reprimanding him, Caroline is a maternal figure for a brother whom she lovingly protects from himself, of course—hence his weakness is a constant refrain. Should it be so surprising, then, if this mongoose watching over the child of the house kills when she feels he is threatened?

This situation is reinforced by what appears to be the essence of Caroline's character in the book: her position as *all-knowing*. The first pages are in this sense emblematic, showing us Sheppard going home to discover that his sister is already in possession of secret information that he has just obtained. Even the thoughts he might formulate are presented to us as *already thought* by Caroline, as if Sheppard occupied the place of a child confronted by the omnipotence of his parents.

Psychoanalysis also allows us to keep them permanently joined—otherwise we would be forced to choose between them—and it is not inconceivable that we are faced here with one and the same character split between two actors in the book. In a psychoanalytic approach, which does not reason in terms of separate characters but in terms of psychic entities, it is the couple Sheppard/Caroline that would be the murderer.[5]

Whether we regard the two characters as one or not, it seems difficult for us in any case, from the standpoint of the unconscious, to imagine that the danger of death would come, in this book, from the indecisive Dr. Sheppard. The only dangerous person, the only decisive—one would be tempted to say phallic—person is Caroline Sheppard.[6] Even more so since, as we shall see, the same conclusion emerges when we examine the structural place occupied by Sheppard and his sister in the literary configuration of Agatha Christie's characters.

If the main dyad is that of brother and sister, any analysis is complicated by the fact that both are shadowed by other characters in Agatha Christie's work who act as their phantasmic doubles.

When we are familiar with the novelist's entire corpus, a first comparison—involving the first part of the dyad, Caroline Sheppard—comes to mind irresistibly: We cannot help but see this sedentary village spinster—who is faintly ridiculous, devoured by curiosity, and who conducts the investigation from her house with the help of a whole network of informers—as a double of Miss Marple, Agatha Christie's other great detective figure.

This comparison of Caroline Sheppard with Miss Marple has been made by several commentators,[7] and by Agatha Christie herself in her *Autobiography*. What is even more surprising for anyone who wants to understand the phantasmic importance of this second role, Christie states here that her favorite character is . . . Caroline Sheppard.[8] So the novel has not only one detective but two, which clarifies the detective-like attitude of the doctor's sister.

The superimposition of Caroline/Miss Marple also tends to position the character of Dr. Sheppard relative to Caroline and to underscore his vacuousness. At the same time, it shows that the text is indeed the narrative of a confrontation between two figures, but that Sheppard, phantasmically, plays a secondary role. It allows us, in effect, to understand that *the real conflict in the book—detective and psychic—pits Poirot against Caroline*.

Here again, curiously, the truth is certainly not concealed. From their first meeting, each falls under the other's spell. Caroline, fascinated by her new neighbor, makes great efforts to meet him. When she learns his profession, she suggests that her reticent brother ask him to conduct the investigation, as if to challenge him. During this investigation, she never stops pressing the doctor with questions so as to be informed of the progress of the inquiries. But Poirot is not passive and assiduously visits the Sheppards' house, showing up several times when the doctor is out making his rounds.[9] Of course, we have reason to think that he is looking for information about Sheppard, but it is also imaginable that he unconsciously senses that Caroline is the repository of a secret other than her brother's guilt.

From the viewpoint of the unconscious, then, the real confrontation does not pit Sheppard against Poirot but Caroline against Poirot. We may even wonder whether *The Murder of Roger Ackroyd* is not, in the first instance, the story of this couple. Otherwise, how can we understand this sentence, one of Sheppard's last: "I meant [my manuscript] to be published some day as the history of one of Poirot's failures!" (XXVII, 253)? This declaration, whose tone is competitive, makes no sense coming from him. It has meaning only if it refers to the detective's great rival, the woman who inspires the text.

If Caroline Sheppard is a phantasmic Miss Marple in this book, her secret importance also makes her the natural representative of Agatha Christie, who has openly constructed these two female characters in her image. As the creator of the story, she is the real murderer of Roger Ackroyd. This might explain the fact that Caroline is considered external to the plot, circulating freely in the book without taking part in it, and excluded on principle—by function rather than character—from the list of suspects.

A second intertextual comparison suggests itself, one that is regularly encouraged by the text but without directly conveying its entire reach: the comparison of Sheppard with Hastings.

The assimilation of Sheppard and Hastings is even stronger since Sheppard merely occupies the post of confidant temporarily. Although *The Murder of Roger Ackroyd* is Agatha Christie's fourth novel, it presents an aging Poirot whose friend Hastings has left to go to Argentina. The couple consisting of Poirot and Hastings will come together again in a whole series of subsequent novels, such as *The ABC Murders* and *Murder on the Links*. So for the space of one novel, just before *Curtain*, preceded and followed by Hastings, Sheppard truly becomes Poirot's double. This assimilation is made explicitly by the detective, who congratulates himself on finding a confidant to whom he can tell the details of the investigation. His enthusiasm grows when he learns that the doctor has composed an account of the affair. This application seems to confirm the manifest function of this confidant: to help Poirot by the confidant's stupidity. Hastings never succeeds in finding the solution to the mysteries he sets out to solve, but his naive reflections voiced in the course of the investigation allow Poirot to succeed in solving them.

This sweetened version of the duo of investigators should not, however, conceal the violence that underlies their relationship. In fact, Poirot is not satisfied with making Hastings or Sheppard his naive confidants: He transforms them into the objects of aggressive release, showering them with sarcasms throughout the investigation. An obscure, almost sado-masochistic hatred is displayed which the text never questions and which gives a singular coloration to this third dyad: a mirror-image couple in which thought can form only in the violence done to the other.

Latent in the novels in which Hastings is the narrator, more explicit in *Curtain*, this violence bursts forth in *The Murder of Roger Ackroyd*, in which Poirot prefigures his attitude in the posthumous work. Not only does he constantly mock his confidant, not only does he come, as in *Curtain*, to accuse him of murder, but he ends by pushing him to suicide, illustrating the violence at work that is the fabric of interpretation.

Interpretation in detective work is first and foremost a death sentence. Taking the logic of all interpretation to its conclusion—to make its object disappear by finding its equivalent in a foreign language—it manages here to kill both the self-proclaimed criminal and that guarantor of transparency who is the confidant. Having done this, it reveals the *pleasure of interpretation*, which is to reduce difference by replacing it with similarity.

This psychoanalytic dissociation of the characters leads us—beyond the factitious opposition between Sheppard and Poirot—to place the character of Caroline (coupled with the doctor or not) in opposition to the character of Poirot. It leads us to reformulate our initial question, asking this time, *Who killed Dr. Sheppard?* The fight to the death between the two detectives reveals itself, in the end, to be a fight between two killers.

For at the moment that Sheppard is declared innocent—simply acquitted by giving him the benefit of the doubt—an essential modification takes place in the story told in the book. It ceases to be the simple account of an investigation and becomes the story of a crime: the slow execution of Dr. Sheppard, the victim of Hercule Poirot's murderous delusion. This is a story told in great detail—unfolding throughout the book but invisible to the blinded reader—of a *murder by interpretation*.

NOTES

Prologue

1. The book has been discussed notably by Roland Barthes, Gérard
   Genette, Algirdas Julien Greimas, and Umberto Eco, as well as by
   numerous writers such as Raymond Chandler and Alain Robbe-
   Grillet. On the eve of his death, Georges Perec was writing an
   article on the subject (*Littérature*, Larousse, 1983, no. 49, p. 15).
2. Agatha Christie mentioned these accusations of cheating in one of
   her autobiographies (*An Autobiography*, Harper Collins Publishers, 1977, pp. 352–353). They are groundless, according to her, if
   one reads the book attentively, since Sheppard carefully calculates
   his literary effects. However, these accusations have been revived
   recently in texts by Roland Barthes and Gérard Genette. On the
   book's initial reception, see Robert Barnard, *A Talent to Deceive:
   An Appreciation of Agatha Christie* (New York: Dodd, Mead and
   Company, 1980), pp. 37–39, as well as Dennis Sanders and Len
   Lovallo, *The Agatha Christie Companion: The Complete Guide
   to Agatha Christie's Life and Work* (New York: Avenel Books,
   1985), pp. 33–34.
3. For this reason we have not refrained from giving the solutions to
   certain Agatha Christie plots, convinced that these were often
   merely masking the real answers.

Part I—Investigation

Chapter 1—The Murder

1. See the list of characters at the beginning of this book. Our reference edition is the Pocket Books edition published by Simon &
   Schuster, Inc., reprinted in 1986. Our references are indicated in
   the form of a Roman numeral indicating the chapter, followed by
   an Arabic numeral indicating the page reference. The absence of a
   reference after a citation indicates that it still refers to the preceding reference.

Chapter 2—The Investigation

1. Flora Ackroyd went to steal the money in a room next to Ackroyd's study. Apprehended by Parker in front of her uncle's door, she pretends to have just left Ackroyd and claims to have spoken with him.
2. Once Hector Blunt admits to glimpsing a feminine silhouette in the park, Poirot deduces that this was Ursula Bourne.

Chapter 3—The Van Dine Principle

1. On the idea of *applying literature to psychoanalysis*, see my earlier works.
2. *The American Magazine*, September 1928, pp. 129–131. This text figures in the anthology *Le Roman criminel* by Stefano Benvenuti, Gianni Rizzoni, and Michel Lebrun (Nantes, France: L'Atalante, 1982), pp. 84–85. It has often been mentioned, notably by Boileau and Narcejac, in *Le Roman policier* (PUF, 1975), pp. 51–55.
3. S. S. Van Dine Op. cit.
4. Ibid.
5. Ibid.
6. Ibid.
7. Ibid.
8. The Van Dine rule, according to which the murderer must not be one of the investigators, is not respected by Agatha Christie.
9. In the story *Victory Ball*, the murderer takes advantage of a masked ball in order to disguise himself—that is, he takes advantage of everyone's use of disguise.
10. This method is minutely described—and theorized—in *The Mirror Crack'd*, in which the inmates of an institution for juvenile delinquents are distracted from the actual murder by the representation of a false murder.
11. In *Agatha Christie: L'Ecriture du crime* (Paris: Les Impressions Nouvelles, 1989), Annie Combes makes this method one of the three great sleights of hand in Agatha Christie. The other two are, in her view, the disguising of the murderer as investigator and as victim.
12. "Witness for the Prosecution," in *"Witness for the Prosecution"*

and Other Stories (New York: Dodd, Mead and Company, 1933).

13. Ibid.

14. The murderer in *Thirteen at Dinner* goes so far as to announce her homicidal intentions to Hercule Poirot.

15. Sigmund Freud, *Jokes and Their Relation to the Unconscious*, tr. by James Strachey (New York: W. W. Norton, 1960).

16. By playing on the basic elements of the truth (a motive, a murderer, clues), several solutions can be employed each time. It is possible for the writer to distract the reader's attention or, on the contrary, to let it linger on sensitive points in the text. And in the latter case, elements of the truth can be disguised or, on the contrary, exhibited with such insistence that the reader will not identify them.

Chapter 4—The Lie by Omission

1. The wedding ring, discovered by Poirot at the bottom of a pond, was given by Ralph Paton to his wife Ursula Bourne. The scrap of fabric was left by Elizabeth Russell during her meeting with her son, Charles Kent, who dropped the quill he used for snorting cocaine.

2. "The reader will perhaps recall a novel by Agatha Christie in which all the invention consisted in concealing the murderer beneath the use of the first person of the narrative. The reader looked for him behind every 'he' in the plot: he was all the time hidden under the 'I.' Agatha Christie knew perfectly well that, in the novel, the 'I' is usually a spectator, and that it is the 'he' who is the actor" (Roland Barthes, *Writing Degree Zero and Elements of Semiology*, tr. by Annette Lavers and Colin Smith [Boston: Beacon Press, 1970], pp. 34–35).

3. This is equally true of *The Murder at the Vicarage*, *Murder in Mesopotamia*, and *The Moving Finger*, which are also written in the first person.

4. On this question of rereading, see Denis Mellier, "Le Miroir policier, ou la question de la relecture dans *Le Meurtre de Roger Ackroyd* d'Agatha Christie," in *Les Cahiers des Paralittératures* (Editions du CEFAL, 1994).

5. We agree on this point with Uri Eisenzweig (*Le Récit impossible*

[Christian Bourgeois, 1986], p. 60) when he takes issue with those—Barthes or Genette, for example—who have reproached Agatha Christie for "cheating" by conjuring away an essential event of the story: "The nondescription of the murder itself is merely one among dozens, even hundreds of others throughout the narrative; you have only to scan a few pages anywhere in the book, knowing that the narrator is also the killer, to realize this."

6. It seems to us that this is the theory of paralepsus in Gérard Genette (*Figures III* [Seuil, 1972], pp. 92–93): "There is another . . . sort of lacuna, of a less strictly temporal kind, that consists not of an elision of a diachronic segment but in the omission of one of the constitutive elements of the situation . . ." Among his examples of paralepsus, Genette cites the incomplete narrative in *The Murder of Roger Ackroyd* (Ibid., p. 212), suggesting that for him paralepsus is possible only if the text finally supplies the missing elements after the fact. For us, the lie of omission is something quite different, a ploy that integrates the set of unsupplied elements, even indirectly or belatedly, into the text.

7. The peculiarity of the lie by omission in this novel comes from its function. Lies by omission that we encounter in the traditional detective story obey the necessity of preserving the mystery as long as possible and creating an effect of surprise. Dr. Sheppard's lies obey the necessity of protecting him.

Part II—Counterinvestigation

Chapter 1—Endless Night

1. Greta has strongly urged Ellie to go for a stroll at "Gipsy's Acre" on the day agreed upon with Michael.

2. Moreover, if only one of the important omissions (for example, the love between Michael and Greta) were supplied, the whole illusion would immediately dissipate.

3. Although the kinship between *The Murder of Roger Ackroyd* and *Endless Night* is unquestionable, it does not seem obvious to us to associate this series, as Dario Gibelli does ("Le Paradoxe du narrateur dans Roger Ackroyd" in *Poetique* [Seuil, 1992], no. 92)

with an early novel by Agatha Christie, *The Man in the Brown Suit*, which he presents as a first attempt to set up the narrator-murderer. Indeed, certain pages are attributed to the murderer, Sir Eustace Pedler, who is keeping his private diary, but this occupies no more than a fifth of the book. The real narrator, whose text takes up the other four-fifths, is Anne, who is perfectly innocent.

Chapter 2—The Paradox of the Liar

1. They have gotten hold of an old photograph taken in Germany, in which Michael and Greta appear together in an unambiguous pose.
2. On this paradox, see my work *Le Paradoxe du menteur: Sur Laclos* (Minuit, 1993).
3. A characteristic instance is *Ten Little Indians*, in which the narrator conveys the thoughts of the characters by selecting them in such a way that the guilty party cannot be recognized. The deception can be even more deliberate, as in *Murder at Hazelmoor*, in which the narrator makes us follow the trajectory of a character from one house to the other, carefully omitting—by an ellipsis as flamboyant as in *The Murder of Roger Ackroyd*— the moment of the murder. In *The ABC Murders*, the narrator alternates the narrative of the investigation with a narrative of the life of the false culprit, who was present in each of the towns where the murders took place.
4. Learning that Dr. Sheppard has written an account of the investigation (XXIII), Poirot asks him to give it to him: "Still somewhat doubtful, I rummaged in the drawers of my desk and produced an untidy pile of manuscript which I handed over to him. With an eye on possible publication in the future, I had divided the work into chapters, and the night before I had brought it up to date with an account of Miss Russell's visit. Poirot had therefore twenty chapters. . . . I left them with him" (XXIII, 228).
5. We might add, to the chapter on structural improbabilities, those raised by Dario Gibelli (op. cit.), who observes that the entire first part of the book is studded with Sheppard's allusions to Poirot's future success and his own failure. How can the doctor know this in advance if he is writing his account day by day? Since he is not

seeking, as we are, another logic to the book, Gibelli simply concludes that the novel is improbable.

6. In general, Agatha Christie's murderers have no trouble confessing, whether directly (*Ten Little Indians*, *Crooked House*) or indirectly (for example, by insulting the investigator as in *The
Mysterious Affair at Styles*, or by trying to flee, in *Cards on the
Table*, or by trying to commit another murder, *The Moving Finger*). This makes Sheppard's silence even more surprising.

Chapter 3—Improbabilities

1. This point would be the same as demonstrating his participation
in the murder. Hercule Poirot's reasoning is rather surprising since
he is content to accuse him without managing to explain the origin
of Sheppard's capital, although he acknowledges that the doctor
loves to speculate (XXVI, 250).

2. Or a pair of gloves, a technique used by the heroine of *Murder at
Hazelmoor*, who, suspecting two women, first pays them a visit,
then returns shortly afterwards thanks to this pretext, in order to
spy on them. When this method proves effective, she uses it again,
a second time, later in the book.

3. It is true that this attitude, given its context, is not completely
unjustifiable. Parker seems to have listened at the door to the last
conversation between Ackroyd and Sheppard, and to have heard
talk of blackmail. Learning of this from the police, the doctor
writes: "I took an instant decision: 'I'm rather glad you've brought
the matter up,' I said. 'I've been trying to decide whether to make
a clean breast of things or not. I'd already practically decided to
tell you everything, but I was going to wait for a favorable opportunity. You might as well have it now.'

"And then and there I narrated the whole events of the evening
as I have set them down here. The inspector listened keenly, oc-
casionally interjecting a question" (VI, 64–65). Sheppard is therefore justified in thinking that the police will interest themselves in
this blackmail business. All the same, it is surprising that he does
not choose to invent another blackmail story, since this is the only
thing that might connect the murder to Ferrars.

4. Georges Arnaud writes humorously in his preface to the novel:
"So well that on the last page, having followed in a critically

faithful spirit Hercule Poirot's explanation demonstrating more clearly than a blackboard exercise that he himself is the guilty party, the criminal, dazzled by logic, hasn't the slightest idea that he might quibble or run away, or draw a gun from his pocket and finish off the witness" (12).

Chapter 4—The Ideal Murderer

1. This accounts, too, for that feeling of frustration when the solution is pronounced at the end of detective novels. As Jacques Dubois observes: "The detective thriller makes its resolution hard to accept. Ordinarily, in the final glory of revelation, the guilty party jumps like the devil out of his box, like the *deus ex machina*. If he is surrounded by an aura of novelty, it is not enough to compensate for the unreality of his naming. There is something arbitrary about it. And we can easily see why. . . . Since throughout the plot the mystery has only thickened, the finale is like a beam of light too sudden and too bright to be entirely tolerable. Above all, since it matters that the name of the guilty party should be unexpected and improbable, the novelist is inclined to assign this role to the least likely suspect. This means that he is obliged to transform point blank an engaging or simply neutral figure into an avowed representative of evil or wrongdoing" (*Le Roman policier ou la modernité* [Nathan, 1992], pp. 143–144).

2. Annie Combes (op. cit., pp. 229–230) is right to separate clues from decoys, which function to open false leads. She also proposes to create a more general term, *detectande*, for regrouping clues and decoys. But she does not go so far as to imagine that clues and decoys can change places according to different readings.

3. Moreover, there are a small number of Agatha Christie's novels with unsolvable endings. The most famous is *Murder on the Orient Express*, in which Hercule Poirot proposes two solutions, one of which—when finally retained—exonerates the murderers. *At Bertram's Hotel* leaves the door open to two readings, the mother of the most likely murderess committing suicide at the last moment by accusing herself of the crime. The female narrator of "The Affair at the Bungalow," a story in the collection *The Tuesday Club Murders* tells a story of theft that has not yet happened,

without saying that she is the protagonist hesitating to commit the crime.

4. "I left the summer-house about nine-forty-five, and tramped about the lanes, trying to make up my mind as to what to do next— what line to take. I am bound to admit that I've not the shadow of an alibi, but I give you my solemn word that I never went to the study, that I never saw my stepfather alive—or dead" (XXIV, 240).

5. According to the investigation made by Poirot (XXIII), and contrary to the secretary Geoffrey Raymond's assertion (VIII), it does seem that Ackroyd had bought a dictaphone. But why should its disappearance, which could be for various reasons, incriminate Sheppard? (XXV, 246)

6. This is not the only case among her novels. In *Murder After Hours*, Hercule Poirot has difficulty solving the mystery because all the clues have been faked by someone who is protecting the killer.

Part III—Delusion

Chapter 1—Crossroads

1. It is true that the Bible also includes detective stories, but without the actual structure of the detective novel.

2. Marie Balmary, *L'Homme aux statues: Freud et la faute cachée du père* (Livre de Poche, 1994).

3. Letter III, in *Oeuvres Complètes*, vol. II, ed. A. Beuchot (Paris, 1830), p. 23. ("Letters written in 1719, which contain the remarks on Sophocles' Oedipus, Corneille's, and the author's.")

4. "Oedipus the King," *Sophocles*, vol. I, tr. David Grene, in *The Complete Greek Tragedies*, vol. 3, ed. Grene and Lattimore (New York: Modern Library, Random House, 1942), p. 56.

5. Ibid.

6. Ibid.

7. Cited in Shoshana Felman, "De Sophocles à Japrisot (via Freud), ou pourquoi le policier?" *Littérature* 49 (Larousse, 1983), p. 37. This article has been an inspiration to me.

8. Ibid.

9. "Analytic theory is perhaps, after all, nothing but the structural consequence of this narrative discovery—lived and written by Freud—of the unconscious imbrication, of the self-subversive implication of the detective in the criminal, of the interpreter in the interpreted, of inquiries of life in the quests of death, of the theoretical logic of the doctor, of the reader, of the speculator, in the oneiric logic of the dreamer" (Ibid., p. 40).

Chapter 2—What Is a Delusion?

1. The hypothesis of Poirot's madness is suggested several times in the book, notably by Inspector Raglan (see, for example, XIX, 193: ". . . he tapped his forehead significantly. 'Bit gone here,' he said. 'I've thought so for some time. Poor old chap, so that's why he had to give up and come down here'"), and then, in their last conversation, by Sheppard ("'You're mad,' I said" [XXVI, 249]).

2. "The difference at the beginning comes to expression at the end in this way: in neurosis a part of reality is avoided by a sort of light, but in psychosis it is remodelled. Or one may say that in psychosis flight at the beginning is succeeded by an active phase of reconstruction, while in neurosis obedience at the beginning is followed by a subsequent attempt at flight. Or, to express it in yet another way, neurosis does not deny the existence of reality, it merely tries to ignore it; psychosis denies it and tries to substitute something else for it" (Sigmund Freud, "The Loss of Reality in Neurosis and Psychosis," *Collected Papers*, vol. 2 [1924], p. 279).

3. "'It is useless to deny. Hercule Poirot knows,'" he says to Parker (XVII, 175). The least we might say is that Poirot is not bothered by any doubt about the accuracy of his construction. "'*Mon ami*, I do not think; I know,'" he declares to Sheppard (XVIII, 191). "'Me, I know everything. Remember that,'" he replies to Geoffrey Raymond, who asks him if he knows Ralph Paton's hiding place (XXIII, 231). And further on: "'And yet I have told you just now that I know everything. The truth of the telephone call, of the footprints on the window sill, of the hiding-place of Ralph Paton—'" (XXIII, 237).

4. One example, among others: It's because he concludes that Paton would have had too many reasons to kill Ackroyd that Poirot

finds him innocent! "'Do you realize that there are separate motives staring us in the face? . . . Three motives—it is almost too
much. I am inclined to believe that, after all, Ralph Paton is innocent'" (XIII, 142–143).

5. "'Do not be too sure that these dead things'—he touched the top
of the bookcase as he spoke—'are always dumb. To me they
speak sometimes—chairs, tables—they have their message!' . . .
He shook his head, puffed out his chest, and stood blinking at us.
He looked ridiculously full of his own importance. It crossed my
mind to wonder whether he was really any good as a detective" . . . (VIII, 89–90).

6. Seeing that Poirot has not managed to find a satisfying solution to
the displacement of the high-backed chair, Sheppard observes,
quite rightly: "'Raymond or Blunt must have pushed it back,' I
suggested. 'Surely it isn't important?'" To which Poirot calmly
replies: "'It is completely unimportant . . . That is why it is so
interesting" (VII, 83–84).

Chapter 3—Delusion and Theory

1. See, for example, the passage on the philosophical fabrication of
"visions of the world" (Weltanschauungen) in Sigmund Freud,
Inhibitions, Symptoms and Anxiety, tr. by Alix Strachey, revised
and edited by James Strachey (London: The Hogarth Press, 1971),
p. 10.

2. Sigmund Freud, "Psychoanalytic Notes Upon an Autobiographi-
cal Account of a Case of Paranoia (Dementia Paranoides)"
(1911), in *Three Case Histories* (New York: Collier Books, 1968),
pp. 181-182.

3. Sigmund Freud, *Delusion and Dream* [on Wilhelm Jensen's
Gradiva, A Pompeiian Fancy] (Boston: Beacon Press, 1956), p.
104.

4. Sigmund Freud, "On the Sexual Theories of Children" (1908),
authorized translation under supervision of Joan Riviere, *Collected Papers*, vol. 2 (London: The Hogarth Press, 1924), p. 65.

5. Sigmund Freud, "Constructions in Analysis" (1937), *Collected
Papers*, vol. 5, p. 371.

6. In his text on Schreber, Freud observes: "And the paranoiac rebuilt the universe, not in a more splendid truth, but at least one

that he might live with again. He rebuilt it by the work of his delusions. *The delusion formation, which we take to be a pathological product, is in reality an attempt at recovery, a process of reconstruction* (op. cit., p. 315, author's italics). It is in this sense that we might also understand Freud's remark in a letter to Ferenczi: "I have succeeded where the paranoiac fails" (cited by Ernest Jones [1910], *The Life and Work of Sigmund Freud*, vol. 2 [New York: Basic Books, 1955], p. 83).

7. Jacques Sédat observes that we find in it one of the characteristic elements of a theory, or even of a real concept: "The condition of an analytic thought inheres in the impossible reference to concepts, to stable gains, to detached results of the very movements of thoughts that have generated them and that would provide material for constructing a theory cobbled together on the model of childhood 'mecanos.' Morover, we should probably go further and state that in analysis there are no (or few) gains, no (or little) progress, no transmissions of a body of knowledge, no orthodoxy and even no concept in the philosophical meaning of the term" ("Théorie et pratique" in *Esprit* 3 (Seuil, 1980), pp. 144–145).

Chapter 4—Delusion and Criticism

1. On the intersections of imaginary and real worlds, see in particular Thomas Pavel, *Univers de la fiction* (Seuil, 1988).

2. Criticizing the psychological commentaries of Jacques Chardonne on the underlying reasons that led the Princesse de Clèves to confess her love for Nemours to her husband, Genette writes: "This explanation is attractive, except for its tendency to forget that Mme. de Clèves's feelings—for her husband as well as for Nemours—are not real feelings but the feelings of fiction and language. That is, these are feelings that exhaust the totality of the statements by which the narrative *signifies* them. To speculate on the [extra-textual] *reality* of Mme. de Clèves's feelings is as chimerical as wondering how many children Lady Macbeth *really* had, or if Don Quixote had *really* read Cervantes" (*Figures II* [Seuil, 1969], p. 86).

3. If the narrator of *every* novel is suspect, then we can no longer rely on any part of the text.

4. Tzvetan Todorov, *The Morals of History*, tr. by Alyson Waters (Minneapolis: The University of Minnesota Press, 1995), p. 90.
5. Here again, see Thomas Pavel, op. cit.
6. In the framework of a truth of disclosure, the text changes through different eras. Therefore, it is not impossible that the murderer might also change, and while Sheppard was indeed the murderer in 1926, he is no longer the murderer today. Having no existence except in relation to the reader's surprise, he can have ceded *later* to another murderer—as the theory and practice of the detective novel have evolved.
7. Freud now finds himself again in a situation analogous to that of the delusional patient. This point appears clearly in the reading of *Gradiva*, in which Freud ends up resembling Norbert Hanold when the former writes: "From two things, one: for we have created a real caricature of interpretation by imputing, to an inoffensive work of art, intentions that its author did not even suspect. We would have thus shown once more how easy it is to find what one is looking for . . ." (Op. cit., pp. 241–242). The passage is entirely characteristic of the binary thinking that rules the logic of adequation, which inspires police investigations. A suspect either *is* the murderer or *is not*. But why should the reading of works comply with such injunctions? Why shouldn't Freud's reading be partially correct, or correct for certain persons, or correct in a certain era?

Part IV—Truth

Chapter 1—Curtain

1. In English, *Poirot's Last Case* or *Curtain*. Another manuscript, *The Last Mystery*, was devoted to Miss Marple's final investigation.
2. See above, I, 3.
3. *Curtain* (New York: Simon & Schuster, Pocket Books, 1975), pp. 254–255. Author's italics.
4. A demon for symmetry, Poirot cannot stop himself from leaving

his signature by taking care to shoot precisely in the middle of Norton's forehead.

5. Author's italics.

6. We understand that Agatha Christie had delayed the publication of the book until after her death.

Chapter 2—The Truth

1. The other testimony is that of Flora Ackroyd (IX, 103), and Poirot proves that she is a liar.

Chapter 3—Nothing but the Truth

1. In our hypothesis, the footprints were left by Paton himself, who never hid the fact that he was roaming around the house that evening. The other footprints may belong to Caroline (this is not incompatible with the text, which suggests "several clearly defined footmarks" (V, 55), but it is also possible that she was careful not to leave any.

Chapter 4—The Whole Truth

1. Rudyard Kipling, *The Jungle Book* (New York: Grosset & Dunlap, Publishers, 1979), p. 154.

2. See, for example, what Buffon says about it: "Its taste for prey is still more lively, and its instinct greater than that of the cat, for it equally hunts birds, quadrupeds, snakes, lizards, insects, attacking in general any living thing, and eating any animal matter. Its courage is equal to the vehemence of its appetite; it is frightened neither by angry dogs nor by cunning cats, and does not even dread snake bites" (*Histoire Naturelle*, in *Oeuvres complètes*, Verdière et Lagrange, 1826 edition, vol. XXII, p. 20).

3. A formulation even more ambiguous since it is not isolated in the work (Caroline, moreover, is qualified as "bad enough as it is" [XIV, 152] and is followed by this sentence: "In fact, all through the case there have been things that puzzled me hopelessly. Every one seems to have taken a hand" (XXVII, 255).

4. To my knowledge, no identical case exists in which a central character would be considered completely beyond suspicion to the

extent that no alibi would be required. Narrative cases similar to *The Murder of Roger Ackroyd*—like *The Murder at the Vicarage* or *The Moving Finger*—show, on the contrary, feminine characters (the wife of the narrator in the first, his sister in the second) suspected of murder and subjected to highly detailed inquiries.

5. Certain passages of the book suggest this—for example, when Sheppard and his sister have just heard Hercule Poirot give them an abstract description of a criminal: "He was silent for a moment. It was as though he had laid a spell upon the room. I cannot try to describe the impression his words produced. There was something in the merciless analysis, and the ruthless power of vision which struck fear into both of us" (XVII, 185).

6. Sophie de Mijolla-Mellor observes, in *Meurtre familier: Approche psychoanalytique d'Agatha Christie* (Dunod, 1995), p. 57: ". . . Even if we acknowledge the relatively artificial character of the text, which requires for the sake of suspense that the reader may not guess that the murderer is the narrator, what characterizes Dr. Sheppard is precisely his extreme normality in relation to which his sister's curiosity seems like a kind of compulsive voyeurism and Poirot's inferences the effect of some sort of madness."

7. Such as Francois Rivière in *Agatha Christie, duchesse de la mort* (Seuil, 1981), p. 112. He also notes the difference in personality between brother and sister: "Sheppard seems to be a provincial snob, affected, not very likable. He does not seem to have even half his sister's temperament, who is the best informed citizen of King's Abbot" (Ibid.).

8. "I think it is possible that Miss Marple was born from the pleasure I had in painting the portrait of Dr. Sheppard's sister in *The Murder of Roger Ackroyd*. She had been my favorite character in the book—an old girl with an acerbic mind, full of curiosity, knowing everything, listening to everything: the perfect amateur detective" (Agatha Christie, op. cit., p. 448).

9. In the theatrical adaptation of the novel, done by Michael Morton in 1928, a romance develops between Poirot and Caroline (see Charles Osborne, *The Life and Crimes of Agatha Christie* [London: Michael O'Mara Books Limited, 1990], pp. 37–38).